The Last

Bruce W. Perry

British slang used in this story:

Barmy: Bonkers, or crazy.

Bloke: A dude.

Bollocks: A vulgar term labeling something as nonsense.

Chuffed: Happy and delighted.

Daft: Stupid in a silly way.

Dodgy: Shady or lacking credibility; ingenuine.

Kip: A short nap.

Knackered: Tiired, fatigued.

Narked: Irritated, ticked off.

Pissed: Very drunk.

Sod: An insult to a man.

Wanker: A masturbater, a general insult or pejorative term.

Welly: As in "give it some welly"; make an effort, try hard at something like sports.

If you liked this book, kindly consider leaving a review on Amazon or Goodreads. This helps writers reach a larger audience and gain recognition for their work.

https://www.amazon.com/dp/B07ZG7K48V

CHAPTER 1: APRIL, 2028

My name is Emma Wallace Blair. I am 28, and I suspect I am the last female left on earth. If you think that sounds gloomy and melodramatic, then you haven't been through what I have, or seen what I've seen.

What I'm talking about is evidence-based. I'm from the north of Scotland; where I'm located now. I've traveled mostly by bicycle, and by junked cars and trucks that have fuel left, and once by horse, but after too long, that hurt my arse, so I let the tired looking mare wander off. I'm writing everything down, "journaling" as it used to be called, mostly not to forget, because remembering is *everything* in this benighted land.

Maybe someday, maybe, someone will find this journal and read it, if there ever *is* a someone.

In the year 2028, I must hold on to my memories. Writing everything down keeps me sane but also has a practical purpose; I can monitor my food, water, and medical supplies, which I do daily.

It has been 540 days since I've seen another human being alive, and uninfected. I've also monitored transmissions from radios and what used to be called "online," and the last time I didn't hear either static or dead air, or see a revolving ball icon, was more than 540 days ago.

There are 365 days in a year so more than 540 is almost exactly 1.5 years. I've been on deep survival mode since October 2026.

I have a routine, if you can call it that. It bears no resemblance to the routine I had before, let's call that period B.C., as in *Before Carnage.* But some habits have remained. As part of my scavenging, which is constant, I horde packaged goods, canned liquids, any non-rotten food, matches, medical supplies, tea bags, and coffee grounds. Most mornings I have a cup of tea or coffee.

I scrounge for everything, and that includes whisky, which I will add to the tea, or drink neat, such as on my birthday. *Here's to me Emma,* I thought on my 28th, which was April 1, 2028.

I was born in 2000, roughly 18 months before September 11, 2001, which was a cakewalk compared with this.

I raise my cloudy old glass of amber whisky to the sky. *And to more birthdays to come.* I cough when it goes down; laugh afterward. Warmth runs down my chest, then rises to my head in a kind of euphoric, giddy vapor. Laughter has a sneaky tone when you're alone. When I laugh it makes me feel, oddly, victorious.

Born in April, that makes me an Aries. An Aries is just supposed to plow forward, no matter what. That pretty much describes what I do now. I've had two birthdays since it happened.

I still have that half-full fifth of whisky, and the three-quarters full bottle of vodka I can use for a disinfectant. Vodka has extremely effective anti-bacterial and anti-viral properties. I expect to find more leftover whisky and vodka, especially whisky. I am, after all, in Scotland.

A fifth of whisky is a bit more than 25 ounces so I have about 12.5 ounces and 18 of vodka remaining.

I keep a weapon beside me *when I lay me down*; now it's a rusty machete. I found this machete in an old falling-down farmhouse, with a bunch of other tools. I took some of them, a tiny axe to help make fires and as another weapon; a can opener to open canned food.

I also have a cricket bat that comes in handy for self defense. I found the cricket bat in an abandoned school, which was at the end of an abandoned road in an abandoned town of an abandoned glen of infected Scotland.

Before, B.C. if you will, I worked for the World Health Organization in the United Nations office in New York City. Emma Blair, virus and pandemic researcher. I last had dinner out with other people, and fiancee Will, 575 days ago. September, 2026. In a Midtown restaurant, with our friends Klara and Jon.

I'm still in the farmhouse, in the countryside on the Isle of Skye, but I'm running out of provisions. What a shame. Springtime, finally, arrived a few weeks ago. The birds dart about; the rising sun shimmers off the wet leaves of the trees. Dew melts into mist as it floats from the green fields, through a warm mixture of sun and breezy air.

I climb a hillside in the morning, after tea and breakfast. What's breakfast? A tin of ham and the stalest brown toast you could imagine. That's a feast these days.

The morning is quiet; the view is beautiful, rolling hillsides and dales. A sea-blue sky with white cottony clouds, as if nothing has changed down below. The loch sits empty of boats beneath me. It goes to the sea, the open ocean, if you keep going, to the Faroe Islands. That must be a bleak island chain now with a sad collection of dead people lying about.

I've seen squirrels, fox, a weasel. It's obvious they're not infected. The strain does not pass to them. One time I saw a herd of deer, wandering unsteadily and aimlessly in a group through a field and a copse of trees.

I wanted to clobber one of them with my cricket bat and axe and cook one up for food, but clearly there was something wrong with them. So I left them alone.

I'm capable of that, you know. Hunting, clobbering an animal for food. I need to consume the meat and the fat, to survive. Vegetarians and vegans need not apply in this situation. But the deer were no good.

The birds aren't infected, the small mammals aren't, that horse that time…I have to watch what I eat…mostly canned goods now and some left-over apples from whoever ran this farm, God rest their soul. I caught fish once in the river nearby, two small trout, chewed down the flesh, bones, everything. I need more of something like that. I can't get weaker.

I'm five foot seven, fighting to stay at 9 stone or about 126 pounds; can't fall below 8 stone.

I've found shampoo and have washed this long unruly red hair a few times. I bath in the river; it's icy and bracing. I dive in and out quick. I don't stay long due to the dangers. Bathing naked leaves me wide open.

I use the cricket bat as a walking stick. In the backpack, which I take up the hill, I bring the axe, a water container that I fill from the river, a little pipe that I play while I'm sitting on a stone.

4

I was terrible in the beginning, when I found this instrument, out of tune, more spitting than blowing. But I can carry a tune now. I make music up; it makes me feel good, carries me away. For a very short time, then I'm back.

I have dog-eared paperbacks that I find in the falling-down houses. Mysteries, crime, histories, I've read it all.

Survival is a full-time job, but somedays only a few hours, so I read more than ever, because there's no one to talk to, nothing to listen to, but a storm at night and the wind through the trees, a broken door banging, the river, gurgling over rocks.

Sometimes, God forbid, I'll hear the moaning and the keening of the doomed sick.

Their final complaint, but the sounds have no sense to them, or humanity, like air escaping from a punctured tire.

I did anything *but* read Before Carnage. I was constantly on the Samsung, tapping out texts, Snap-chatting, checking my email. Staring at the screen, as if it was me mum. Randomly reading web pages, endlessly following threads, plowing through content on Netflix, Facebook, then back to the cell. I realized I was doing it; it felt impulsive and imbecilic, after a while. I don't miss it.

Sitting on my rock, on the top of my hill, I look up. Shit! Shit, shit. Reivers come up the slope toward me, a horde of them. I think they've spotted me. No place to hide.

CHAPTER 2

I hoist the backpack; it's at least 20 pounds with the water. I jog heavily down the hill, away from the pursuers. There must be ten infected people, both men and women.

They stagger across the hillside towards me, weirdly coordinated, like a jittery flock of demented birds. They make that skin-crawling noise I've heard, a humming or muttering. You can't call it communication. They're dressed in rags and grimy clothes, with filthy, gap-toothed faces.

Ugly, ugly!

I have no choice but to head back to the farmhouse. I've been down this road before; they are relentless, however much I don't want them to find my farm. I can't just run off, stumble into the woods, because I'm not guaranteed to lose them. I still have my stuff at the farmhouse! I can't just leave it there! No abandoning, no waste!

I run faster over the hummocky grass, kind of bent over

with my pack, clutching the cricket bat like a spear. They're gaining on me; they make a kind of Vee formation, with the greasy lout in front, the hair sparse but wild, fists clenched, unclenching, enraged eyes plastered open. Keyed on me.

Finally, I go from thick grass to gravely road. My speed picks up; so do they, *Shit!* They're only 25 yards behind.

If I can only split them up. They've already left a few stragglers.

You cut a snake's head off, the tail still moves, the jaws can still inject venom. The reivers are the opposite; once they split up, commonly fewer than five, they become useless, comically adrift, mindlessly plodding about.

They are completely dependent on the whole, like a multi-celled organism with some key cells flaking off. The effect is sudden. They wander about vacuously, then finally collapse, like any old sicky, often in less than 24 hours.

I've been watching, cataloging the symptoms. They're not all the same.

I get to the driveway. I look behind me. Still the lout with four others behind. He's got a leader-of-the-cretins doltish grin. I've got ten yards to go, but I'm badly outnumbered.

I don't know whether I can beat them to the front door, rip it open, slam it shut in time.

I grit my teeth, suppressing the terror. Then, at a full sprint, I weave through this roped maze I've created, like carrot rows in a garden. But wider between the lanes. It's my last line of defense.

CHAPTER 3: NYC, SEPTEMBER 2026

"I say it's a robot apocalypse. Artificial intelligence run amok. They just turn stuff off to collapse our systems first, then reemerge, armies of them. Steel troops with advanced chips for brains."

That was the dinner in New York City, what seems like ages ago. Indian food, happy chatter, candlelight. A heady, winey conversation. No clue what was coming around the corner. Not a bloody clue.

It breaks my heart to think of how innocent and naive we were; what I've lost since then, as in everything. Jon Lloyd, my fiancee Will's friend, spent dinner pontificating about what would cause the end of the world, as if he knew anything about that

Will sat across from him, our friend Klara, Jon's young wife, kitty-corner. Table of four, lights low, two near-empty wine bottles, curry-stained plates passed around, Manhattan pulsing with promise and frenetic life just outside the windows. I hate to think of what happened, just weeks later. The city reduced to terror and chaos, then a graveyard of 500-foot tombstones.

Parlor talk before the castle is burned, pillaged, the occupants slaughtered.

Jon continued on: "Robots will write their own software at the speed of light, then wipe us all out as superfluous." He worked for a startup in Brooklyn, same place as Will. They figured we'd all get rich from the I.P.O., move to some island in Indonesia, escape the dull nine-to-five for good.

"Laser weapons," he added for emphasis.

"No," Will said. He had long black hair and a mustache, looking a bit likably unkempt. I loved him, that man. He pursued me with all his heart, a bit too smart for his own good, but a modern romantic.

"It would have happened already, if it was going to, this robot apocalypse. Except for manufacturing and maybe Wall Street trading, I find the A.I. stuff, in fact, a bit overblown."

People were having this conversation a lot then, as if they were laying bets on horses. It seems the height of complacency, to my mind now, cheerful banter about what causes the end of humanity, with this implied attitude that it will never happen, because the thinking on that topic, if it ever got the proper respect that it deserved, would inspire such fear as to render everyone silent.

Will pushed on. "Plus, all you have to do is pull the plug on the 'bots. The bits and bytes need electricity. I think it will be a nuclear mistake. Near misses happen all the time; we just don't hear about them. Some knucklehead misinterprets a digital signal. Thinks it's an incoming ballistic missile. Remember what happened in Hawaii? Everyone got a text message that a missile was on its way; T minus ten seconds and counting to the mushroom cloud. People were shoving their kids down into sewer holes."

Everyone got quiet for a second, calmly chewing their dinner food, all except for Will of course. "The U.S., in all likelihood, responds massively. And 90 percent of the human race is wiped out."

We thought that was unthinkable then. Try 99.999 percent, or thereabouts.

"Asteroid hit," Klara chirped, having to get her two cents in. I think she majored in something like astronomy; now she was teaching high school and planning to get pregnant. Least, that's what she told me. I think she was probing me; she wanted to talk babies. I didn't; me and Will weren't there yet. We weren't married, but boy was that the writing on the wall!

But I wasn't going to let the lad knock me up and force the issue, whatever I wanted deep down.

These things take some thought beforehand, this making of babies.

"Well, it could happen," Klara said. "One rock just drifted through the solar system. The length of a soccer field and the width of a Mack truck. They say if it struck our planet and crashed into the sea, it would create a tsunami 300 meters high…"

"That's 990 feet, for the rest of you…" I said.

"Yeah, almost a thousand feet high. A wave that would inundate a whole continent. Like that…" She snapped her fingers. "Instantaneous. Only a few people monitoring the ocean would know; it'd be traveling too fast. We'd drown in our beds."

"Oh!" Everyone groaned in unison. Glasses and silverware clinked as people returned briefly to food. The undercurrent was, that comment was hitting too close to the bone.

"Sounds more like a Bruce Willis movie to me," Jon said, with good-natured admonishment. "Send those Top Gun guys up there to blow the thing up." Klara moped, thinking her theory was dismissed in a disrespectful manner.

Jon turned to me. "Emma, I bet you have an opinion on this. I can guess. You work with germs. What do you think? What gets us in the end?"

"I think…" I rotated the stem of my wine glass, thinking, wondering if I was even going to contribute to this sophomoric debate. "A pandemic is likely…Nothing extinction-level."

"You don't think so?" Jon wanted something extinction-level, as if anything less was disappointing. Lacked sex appeal.

"Millions of deaths, sure. That could happen. Like the Spanish flu. But let's not trivialize an outbreak, just because it's not extinction level. A pandemic could kill people we know. Anyone with a weakened immune system. It would sweep through the population, leaving a lot of victims. It takes time to develop a vaccine or antitoxin. It could be a strange pathogen, something emergent. Permafrost melts, bacteria still alive…more likely carried by a bat…"

They listened to me, because this is what I did for a living. Then Klara heaved a sigh.

"Does anyone want dessert?"

"What do they have?" Then everyone was fighting over the dessert menu, and we dropped the apocalypse options, almost as quickly as the discussion was brought up.

That was two weeks before the outbreak. The utter catastrophe that unfolded in my home at that time, New York. Ten million people.

I still remember Will's face that night of the dinner. I can't get him out of my mind. We go back to my apartment downtown. I loved that apartment, sparsely furnished but with a nice kitchen overlooking a mew clogged with flowers and vines. You could go up onto the roof and I placed one of the kitchen chairs up there, to sit in the springtime sun.

I picture that apartment now, but only empty and enfolded in the terrible, spectral silence of a dead city.

But it was evening then. We walked into my apartment and quickly shed our clothes. Nudity bathed in angled illumination of streetlights through a partly shaded window. Will had a terrific behind on 'im. He was ready for me; took me in his arms and ran his hands over my breasts and arse. He kissed me down my white neck, then we fell into the pile of cozy covers on my bed. Me on top. Music playing faintly in the background, a female blues singer, from another apartment.

Just two weeks later, as I said, the curtain came down.

I get sad, a chill comes over me, when I think I may never be held by another human being. A person's warmth, that's what I crave. Will got sick like the others. It began when he woke up one morning and forgot where he worked.

CHAPTER 4

"It's just a temporary brain lock." In my kitchen, I shoved some bacon and eggs in front of him, sitting at the table.

"No, I swear, I woke up and didn't know where I was, where I worked…I didn't even drink that much last night, right?"

"Right."

He slowly pushed the plate away, a distasteful grimace, as if I'd served him dog food. That wasn't like him. There was a sick pause.

"You know, you take the D train," I said. "You work in Brooklyn."

"I do?" He stood up; he was sweating. On his face, the forehead. I didn't like the look of 'im. His expression was uncommonly bewildered, dismayed.

I put my palm on his wet forehead.

"You're a bit feverish. You should lie down." He wandered

into the next room, seeming lost. I was worried, more than the least bit. "You're not fucking with me now, are you?"

A full 30 seconds, then "No way." I looked down, then I started eating his breakfast. I heard, "Can you go and get me some...Motrin...get the fever down. The Walgreens, on the corner..."

Well fuck, he remembered that, I recall thinking.

"Sure," I said, wiping my hands with a towel, swallowing some chewed up eggs and bacon. I walked into the bedroom. He stood there staring out the window. Traffic, construction noise. The rush hour in full bloom.

"You still don't remember where you work."

"Starlight Systems."

"Correct."

He gave me this deadly serious look. "I had to look it up, on the computer, based on the description you gave me. I truly didn't know where I work. I don't know anyone I work *with*."

"Jon," I said. That was his present best friend.

He shook his head. "No."

"Jon Lloyd..."

He lurched toward me, with a vulnerable desperation in his eyes.

"Now lie down...I'll get you that ibuprofen. Do you have a headache? What did you eat yesterday? Food poisoning's pretty bad. Did you have any Romaine lettuce?"

"The usual. Oatmeal. A bagel and peanut butter. Steak and salad. No Romaine, as far as I know."

"Do you feel nauseous?"

"No. But I feel...different." He lay back on the bed and clutched a pillow to his face. "More than tired," he said, muffled. "A malaise. I can't remember anyone I work with, or my telephone number, or my social security..."

14

He was panicked, so I sought to calm him down. He was in the grip of something.

"You know how it is, the brain works in mysterious ways. We're just saturated with information. How can we remember all this crap? The other day, I couldn't recall an actress' name, for the life of me. It was Scarlet Johansen. I think we naturally filter some of it out."

"Where do *you* work?"

"You don't know?"

"No!"

I paused, a bit miffed. I did think he was fucking with me. Cognitive impairment, it doesn't work this fast.

"The World Health Organization. I have to go to work, by the way, in half an hour. Do you want me to call in?"

"No, go. But I do need that ibuprofen."

"I'll be right back."

I went down four flights of stairs. I had no elevator; this helped keep me fit, and the rent down. I went outside, clouds, breezy, cabs, noise. People moving about on the sidewalk. I was relieved, felt a modicum of normal again. Outside can do that. He was freaking me, himself, out.

I wanted to walk longer, for a break, but a Walgreens was only three and a half blocks away, on Seventh Avenue. I made that walk briskly, dodging people along the way, thinking, *it's only the flu, and it's clogged up his brain, but that wasn't like him, to panic about being sick. The alarm was…genuine.*

Entered the Walgreens, unpleasant fluorescent light, disinfectant smell. A long line of people in front of the counter, clutching boxes and bags. I hunt around for "Cold Remedies, Headaches," find what I'm looking for. Make a selection, Motrin and Advil, go back to the end of the line.

Tired lady behind the counter bends to a microphone and

says, "Help with the registers up front." I don't want to wait.

A guy, blandly dressed in a full-length beige rain coat, slept on gray hair, turns and looks at me, then down at the boxes he's holding. They're toothpaste and cortisone gel. For some reason, he reminds me of the "I'm mad as hell and I'm not going to take it any longer" actor. His expression is instantly familiar as Will's: bewildered, afraid, latent consternation.

"What *is* this?" he says to me, referring to the boxes. Then he looks up and walks and stumbles straight into an aisle of shelves, as if he has no control over his legs and locomotion, knocking pharmaceutical product onto the floor. A woman in line squeals, puts a hand over her mouth, leaves the line for the exit, still clutching store items.

Suddenly people are walking away from the line, blindly, a startled flock of pigeons in the park. The guy in the raincoat is lying on the floor.

Heart attack, I'm thinking, *no, seizures*.

"Do not leave the store without paying for that!" the register woman yells, unheeded. I look down at the guy; no one helped. The store is chaos as people bump and shove. I make a motion towards him, then he gets up slowly and walks away, vacantly, muttering to himself.

I slap a ten on the counter and walk out with my goods, certain that Walgreens won out on that transaction. When I get outside, something has changed. A Yellow Cab screeches to a halt because some dolt walks right into its path.

The bumper brakes just short of his knee and he stands and gazes about in the middle of Seventh like a awed toddler. The avenue is full of people, some in a hurry to get somewhere, others drifting about aimlessly. Traffic stopped; sirens sound. The crisis appears multi-sourced, not just one gangbanger brawl or one high-rise fire.

16

Now I just want to get back to the apartment, and when I do, clutching the two medicine boxes, I find Will lying on his back on the bed, eyes glued to the ceiling. When he turns to look at me, it's *he* that, strangely, *I* don't know now, the alien and glassy eyes, frozen in bewilderment and fear.

CHAPTER 5

The big greasy guy stands there, ugly mouth agape. He's pressed against a rope I'd strung up across the backyard. The rope marks off a lane, perpendicular to other strands of rope that I'd staked to the ground. A simple but usable maze.

The man no longer resembles anything close to an intelligent species. He doesn't have a clue which way to go, in his pursuit of me. I got 'im where I want him, confused and at a standstill.

I wind up with the cricket bat and let him have it, with relish, right in the face. There's a snap of cheekbone and he falls backward and crashes to the ground. I want to finish him off with another blow, but the damage has been done. I've split them up; big victory for me.

The others lean against the ropes, muttering and gazing myopically at the sky. I've seen it before; the behavior has various permutations and patterns. Some reivers stare endlessly upwards, as if awaiting the rapture from their God, who long ago forsake them. Others wander into the woods with no more purpose than a toddler seeking sensations and warmth.

They will all topple over soon, lie down, not get up. They can't feed themselves, unless they're in a group, as I said, greater than four, "group feeding," which is another way of saying a rending and tearing that would do justice to a flock of vultures or a pack of hyenas.

Alone, they couldn't even open a bag of potato chips; they'd have to be hand fed.

I close and latch the back door behind me, lean on the brick wall inside, near my kitchen. I take long deep breaths, listening to my own gasps. Inexplicably, I begin crying, cheeks soaked, stricken face turned to the black scorch marks on the wall.

I shut down the tap almost as quickly as it flows, however; no time for self-pity. But that was a close one, my closest scrape in six months.

I look out the back window through a screen, and I still see two reivers, a male and a female, the only ones left of the marauding pack. Vengefully, I want to clobber them, administer the *coup de grace*, a bit of the Marquess of Queensberry with the cricket bat. But I almost pity them for their helplessness.

Due to the blow I rendered to their leader, I take a kitchen knife and cut another notch in the handle of the cricket bat. He was number seven.

Around me are arranged stacks of dried-milk boxes, scavenged from a shop near the wharf at Portree. Just add boiling water from the river, and I have a taste like chalk but a legit source of protein and calcium. I'm running low on matches. I have a flint, but it has dulled. You don't truly appreciate matches, until you are down to your last ones.

Everything can be scavenged; nothing is useless.

I have to pee, out of acute stress, so I go outside and squat in the grass. The grass is long and lush; *it* isn't sick, helped along by the ever present Scottish rain. I peer around guiltily, out of an old habit I haven't been able to shake. One of the few upsides of a 99.999 percent pandemic is that I can squat down comfortably, beyond the scope of prying eyes, wherever I want.

One of the reivers has collapsed by the edge of the trees; she lies there in a fetal position. The other perambulatory one is gone. The guy I dropped to the canvas is still out on the grass. I return to my house.

Fear for my life has also emptied me, so I go into the kitchen. I keep a sack of potatoes and a sack of oatmeal in the sealed, no-longer-cold fridge, to keep away from the mice. Those bulletproof pests are unaffected by the virus, as are many other creatures.

I pre-made some oats and potatoes so I glob some onto a plate and season it from a Morton Salt box, then dig in. I look around, chew slowly, savoring, swallow a mouthful. I'm relieved not to see some demented face in the window.

Months ago, I taught myself to eat slower, digest efficiently, savor, don't wolf as if it's my last supper, even if that outcome remains a possibility.

I had an apple earlier for breakfast; I've searched for wild berries, but haven't found many yet. Not too many wild apples left in the Highlands, which really is a windswept, largely treeless landscape. Now deathly quiet, but for those winds coursing across the moors and headlands.

I mix the oats and taters up with dandelion greens; the easiest food I can find. Must get vitamin C; must prevent scurvy. The greens have plenty of C, as do the apples. The first symptom of scurvy is fatigue, and the last thing I need is another drag on my system. I have to stay one step ahead.

I scrape the crusty mush off the bottom of the plate, chewing the last of the dandelion stalks. Nothing is wasted. The food makes me sleepy. I steal a look outside; two robins flit amongst the few stately trees, a raven flaps overhead. The sky is gun-metal gray and darkening. The clobbered leader still lies by my maze.

I go outside, maneuver to his legs, pull him across the lawn to the edge of the woods, then roll him down into a shallow gully, full of wet leaves.

I don't want to lure another pack to my yard, by leaving bodies around. The female lies nearby, as if dropped out of a tree. The familiar fetal position, eyes open. She goes into the gully as well. She's got dirty blond hair, since gone feral and wiry, fair, filthy skin, and she can't be five years older than me.

Granted, she was once someone's daughter, perhaps sister, best friend, soulmate. She might have been brilliant, a scholar, Prime Minister material. When everyone's dead, the whole population, however, pity and sorrow lose their individuation and potency, and with that, their power to move.

I could have been her. Down the body rolls, limbs clubbing the underbrush, the leaves and mud sticking to the pink shirt and the matted hair.

I turn and walk slowly back to the stone house.

The evenings are the worst, the oncoming darkness of the countryside. Silence and loneliness settling down like an anvil. The only music I have is the pipe. I rely on sleep to flee the dreadful quiet. Tonight, I allow myself a small fire in the fireplace of the back patio, and a whisky. Toast the victorious warrior.

This, I have plenty of, Laphroig, 15-year-old Scotch,

smooth as silk. Amber, aromatic, five ounces neat, in a real glass. I don't know whether the book I drop in my lap is Blake or Byron, because I drain the dram and fall asleep in an instant.

Outside the window, it's all black velvet, the starlight cloaked by clouds, and somewhere in the dark landscape, legions of the wandering lost.

CHAPTER 6

I dream of Will; I wake up in the middle of the night. I think he's lying beside me. When I realize he's not, my chest is clutched by an icy blast whose source is my own soul. I get up from the chair, wander through the darkness to my bed, same floor, and climb onto the mattress and pull a blanket over my head.

He still seems beside me, at least by my own invention.

I met Will in Edinburgh, Scotland, four years ago at a professional conference. The U.K., 2024. We struck up a conversation on the fourth floor of my hotel, in front of the elevator. I found him cute, and a little nebulous, full of far-reaching ideas and crack observations. An engaging young American with a black mustache and shy, inquisitive manner.

I was wearing a cute dress that showed off some curves, and I could tell I'd caught his eye. I was a lean, pretty red head. I'm leaner now, believe you me. The eagerness and innocence that might have grabbed the attention of the males back then has since been wrung out of me by dire circumstances, but I could always be wrong.

As Robert Burns wrote, I paraphrase, if only we could see ourselves through the eyes of others.

After a brief, awkwardly funny conversation, we found ourselves out walking on Princes Street, one of the city's main boulevards. It was sunny; there must have been a stretch of prior gloom, because everyone was collapsed in the thick grasses of the city parks, luxuriously soaking in the sunlight.

It was a city of young people and tourists, and for some reason, largely young lads careering around drunk and asking for handouts. Having come the day before from America, Will mentioned he wasn't used to seeing young white men as the homeless.

We were both in the mood to get outside and avoid the responsibilities that had brought us to Edinburgh in the first place. Mine, I was supposed to be sitting in stale conference rooms at an international conference center listening to research papers on various aspects of modern pandemics.

Unfortunately, from the perspective of now, none of the research was prescient enough, focused, as it was, on only existing pathogens and known dangers such as swine flu in China, and bat vectors for emergent viruses in Central Africa.

If I'd heard one paper or theory, I'd heard them all. There wasn't a single paper or even a mention of a super contagion whose initial symptoms were acute and worsening dementia and memory loss.

At the moment, I recall guilt at blowing off some of the talks, but I'd also met a smashing lad. We ended up in a cafe on the street. I ordered white wine and rapidly got pissed. He drank beer. We sat in the sun and it was divine.

24

I didn't want to be anywhere else; we seemed enclosed in a bright, comforting bubble. It was quite enough to be in a cafe on a boulevard bathed in sunlight, watching a river of humanity stream past on the sidewalk.

Soon, the sun gleamed from behind the toothy rows of Edinburgh's soiled rooftop chimneys. Dusk bloomed on the horizon. We chatted and walked aimlessly. We laughed at the Wellington statue and the construction cone someone had placed on his head.

Among other problems of the world we attempted to solve that afternoon, we argued about when global warming would really kick in. What its affect would be on Scotland, which appeared based on my homeland loyalties to be a pretty good place, with its cool airs and northern latitude, to "ride it out." Little did I know...

After walking for about five miles, we decided to hike up Calton Hill, where sat the Scottish version of the unfinished Parthenon, affectionately called "Edinburgh's Disgrace."

It wasn't a disgrace to me; I think of it as a cherished memory.

A line of people plodded up the long hill to catch the sunset. In the near distance was Holyrood Park and the cliffs and ridges of Arthur's Peak, so impressive for being a sizable mountain for just outside a city center. The incandescent yellow gorse blooming over the mountain's flanks–Scottish broom–was gorgeous. It smelled sweet of coconut.

Will clamored on top of the stone foundation of the National Monument, there are no steps, then offered me his hand. He boosted me up and we sat on the cool stone with a bunch of other people and watched the sun set.

The old gray buildings, the lush green of the parks and the trees, led down to the dark blue waters of the North Sea.

I looked at Will and smiled, and he let his arm go around my shoulder. I'd only known him for about five hours. Then we kissed. I laughed and he raised his eyebrows sensitively, assuming I was making fun of his technique. But it was a warm happy laugh, then I reassured him by leaning over and kissing him again.

The memory is scorched on my brain. We wandered down Calton Hill in the dark, with all the other young revelers, I recall, as I lay in the dark in the Skye farmhouse, alone. Oh so alone.

I didn't let him sleep with me that night. Probably didn't want him to assume I was some type of easy lay; now I wish I did. But that came later, since we both already lived in New York City.

I close my eyes in the pitch black, listening to the wind strike against the window glass, and try to sleep.

CHAPTER 7

I go outside to scavenge some more, after a cup 'a tea. Although I prefer my tea white, the milk I make with powder makes the brew taste chalky and bitter, so I drink it black.

I wear the backpack, grab the cricket bat, and hike back down to Portree. There are still plenty of empty homes to search, the problem being also random packs of reivers, made up of normal Portree residents. Now they're infected; this is what has prevented me from living in the town in the first place, the constant presence of the marauding sick.

The residue of the dream about Will lingers with me. I gaze out on the loch. It's a cold blue with white wavelets, but I know close to shore you can find turquoise waters shot through with sunlight.

I keep imagining a fishing vessel will sail in some morning, silent and majestic. But the waters remain empty and primordial.

It comes in a wave; a feeling that I want Will back, the deep sorrow engulfing me when I realize that this can never happen.

I recall his qualities, as I stand and gaze at the loch some more. Will probably would be outfitting a boat right now, if he were here with me. Better with his hands and more of an engineer than me. Of course, I still consider the possibility of boating down the coast, for later when I'm not just surviving hour by hour, if that time ever comes.

Will and I never fought. I didn't have episodes like that to regret now. It wasn't that we were somehow superior to other couples; arguing just wasn't in our natures. In Will's case, he certainly would debate a point vigorously, but I got the idea that he was afraid of showing me a bad side of himself by fighting over petty matters.

He might have viewed arguing as betraying weakness. At any rate, we experienced more bliss than conflict and I needed more years with the lad. Many more.

After sweeping me off my feet in Edinburgh, an unconsummated tryst, we returned to New York. Within a month, I'd vacated my Queens flat, and moved in with him in Brooklyn. He had a one-bedroom apartment in a neighborhood not far from the famous bridge. Moving in was my initiative. He was as indecisive about big life moves as any man.

We had jobs, me at the U.N., him at Starlight Systems, and jogging together through parks and other urban landscapes, which was followed in the evening by Thai or diner food. We had the urban denizens' disinclination to cook most of the time.

Man, has that changed. I'd last three weeks maximum without my barebones, but nutritious meals; three days without a reliable water supply. Back then, we were city people, targets of contempt by the silent masses of preppers who dwelled far

28

from the seething urban hordes. Now *I'm* a kind of prepper.

I've learned, you don't need survival skills...until you do.

In New York, I went to the gym more than Will did. Again, good thing I did. I carry muscle as a thin layer of armor all over my body, giving me the power to swing the cricket bat when it counts most. Despite the fashion (now of course, obsolete) among females, I never thought it was too smart or becoming, to be too skinny.

Will didn't go to the gym, because he didn't think it would be fun. Going into a room full of mostly strangers and hoisting bars and balls of iron made no sense to him. And there was me, swinging a kettlebell and admiring my latissimus dorsi in the mirror afterward.

Not that it made me stronger than Will. He had the foundation of a good bod on him, just not the willpower or the vanity.

Down below, briefly carried away by memories, I see the small collection of buildings and the wharf area that is Portree. In the distance, I don't notice the decay as much. Many of the buildings are still gaily colored. A pallor of thin gray smoke lays over other parts of the town, the result of random fires that start and burn themselves out.

After about six months of living together, we pooled our salaries and moved into an apartment in the Chelsea section of Manhattan. It was the closest thing to heaven on earth, for a young couple with no other responsibilities but to work and have fun, until a species-shattering event brought an abrupt and violent end to our youthful bliss.

Will used to say, "Don't beat yourself up over failures assuming they're all your fault, and don't gloat over successes as if only you achieved them."

So I try not to suffer with guilt now, the ultimate survivor's guilt.

He also used to say, "You can love your work if you learn to stuff the toxic people who also work there." It was the toxic *pathogen* he didn't see coming.

I look out at the loch and once again half expect to see fishing boats making a placid progress toward the wharfs, the mountainous island of Raasay just across the hard blue water. A moss green mat covers its smooth slopes, not many trees or any signs of old human development. I dream about making a go of it in Raasay, where there would be no reivers, but I would rapidly run out of food. Nothing much grows over there; you can't exist solely on dandelions and occasional bunches of raspberries.

Neither is there much or any wood to burn in the winter, or a clean source of water. It's a non-starter, I think, loping downhill with my pack and scanning the horizon for marauders.

It would just be another place to be lonely, and then a chill runs through me as I imagine dying alone on Raasay, without another soul knowing I was there. I readjust the backpack with an angry shrug of the shoulders, tapping a nearby rock with the cricket bat. These gloomy ruminations get me nowhere.

I enter a neglected street that leads to the wharfs, and what used to be rows of buildings that were considered downtown. I steel myself. It's in the Old Town where I have to be most attentive. *Watch your back, Emma.*

CHAPTER 8

The death of organized society shows first on the roads. No one to repair the potholes and washed-away shoulders and clear the fallen trees and branches. A car hasn't taken this road in almost two years, I think. Weeds sprout through the cracks in the concrete, which is no better than a gravel path, but at least I know where it leads.

I stop and listen; nothing but wind through trees. Sunlight blazes through a lattice of tree branches, strikes and bathes my face. The sky is an empty as the loch itself, pale blue and unmarred by a Boeing or Airbus contrail in countless months. I keep going.

Around any bend I can come upon reivers, so I preplan escape routes. Up that path there through the woods to the hotel that used to be called Cullin Hills. I can hide there; I've already explored their kitchen, several times. Being on my lonesome has one advantage. I'm the only rational being in this region scavenging for food, as far as I know. No competition.

I tend to walk on egg-shells during these risky daylight excursions. I'm bolder than I was before, however, when I hid all day. I pass homes, some burned down by random lightning strikes, gas leaks, a stove left on. I've been in some of them before. Nothing edible was left unless it was rotten. It's been so long since refrigerators were turned off and humans made an effort to preserve food.

I'm looking for canned foods and oats, potatoes, and rice without mold. Meat, I'm always searching for preserved meat. Liver would be better, and smoked salmon, which used to be produced in local salmon farms right out on the loch.

If you live on rice and have no meat you can contract a B-vitamin deficiency disease called beriberi. That would mean a slow, agonizing death. Must find eggs, meats. Must keep taking my B's. I haven't had eggs in ages. The B-vitamin loss can bring on a crippling fatigue that means not being able to escape reivers. Good thing...for now...I have leftover vitamin supplements.

I head for what's left of the restaurants and food shops. I know finding them is a life or death issue for me; I'm also searching for new supplies of supplements.

The virus, and the loss of humans, has resulted in more than just an abundance of sick deer. The cows have gone wild; hence, in the back of my mind is a cow and sheep hunt. One kill, if I manage the harvest right, will feed me good for more than a week.

I'll see a cow or a sheep in the distance sometimes, meandering down headlands. They've been attacked by the reivers; I know they have. I haven't seen any sick ones though. Unlike deer, I'm not convinced they can contract the virus.

The broken street climbs into what's left of downtown

32

Portree. A shattered marina lies beneath the wharf where I walk. Two-thirds of the boats have sunk but are still roped to pilings. They're visible below surprisingly clear, teal waters, lapping back and forth against a seaweed- and mud-covered wall.

Other vessels, fishing, sailing, and recreational, are wind- and weather-battered, but washed up reasonably intact on the green, slimy cement shoreline. Opposite this battered fleet of boats, across the street, are the decayed clapboard facades of dwellings that used to be restaurants, hotels, and B & Bs.

Many of the windows are broken in the buildings facing the sea, the doors bashed in, the facades scorched by old fire marks. I stop, scan the whole area; the coast seems clear. Once crammed with tourists and fishermen, the street is empty but for the hulks of abandoned vehicles. Already searched by me.

I walk to a restaurant that used to be called Sea Breezes. Old decayed restaurant buildings are all over the place. They are a potential gold mine, as long as I remain undetected by reivers. Stopping at the door, I look around the ghost town of Portree. Nothing. I give the door a shove, step in.

CHAPTER 9

The room smells gamey, a sweet scent of rot that buoys my hopes of finding food. The dining room is small, tables and chairs up-ended, an accompanying smell of mold as shattered glass windows have let the rains in.

A blackboard hanging on the wall is still scrawled with a finale of specials: Caesar salad, tomato bisque, salmon almondine. My stomach growls and suggestiveness has suddenly starved me. Desserts: chocolate torte and apple crisp.

As a stare at the board, the door slams shut. I whip around brandishing the cricket bat; it was only the wind, but I still feel on the razor's edge. One door, partly ajar, leads to the kitchen; another to a connected hotel, which I may search next. I set the pack down, unfasten the top, and enter the kitchen. A long grill ossified with black grease; a sink crammed with used pots and pans. The floor is wet and slimy, probably burst pipes and condensation. Rows of unfinished paper tickets are still clipped above the grill.

In the corner of the large kitchen is a standing freezer and industrial-sized fridge, which I head for. The freezer is filled with melt water and floating food, mostly expired lamb chops, meat patties, and salmon and steak filets. Holding on to hope, I do a quick assessment; no cigar. Everything's probably saturated with e coli and salmonella, even if I cook them thoroughly, too risky. I shut down the freezer lid, and the fetid odor contained therein.

On to the fridge. It too is warm, predictably, but filled with drinks. Unopened bottles of Irn Bru Scottish soda. I take one, bang the top on the stainless steel counter a couple of times to pry off the bottle top, then guzzle the delicious sweetness. It's flat, but tastes brilliant.

There's also a gallon jug of water; that goes into the backpack–I can also use the empty jug later–along with a couple of Irn Bru. I can't take them all, I'll come back for them later.

I quickly go to the kitchen door and look past the dining room to the street. No movement. The door is partially ajar and moves imperceptibly to gusts of wind off the loch. I return to the kitchen, look up, and see a high shelf holding a row of food containers. Standing on a chair, I find Morton Salt, an extra large jar of pickles, a box of cocoa powder, and mayonnaise, mustard, relish, and olive oil. I stash the salt and the cocoa, the condiments have spoiled with blobs of green mold floating on top of their contents. I'm so anxious and rushed I fling the Mayo and relish aside and they smash on the concrete floor.

I break open the pickles and start devouring them; the leftovers I stash. I still have room for the olive oil.

The backpack is really heavy now, unrealistic to add anything to it. I hoist the pack, snake my shoulders into the straps, and I'm back out into the dining room. Out the window, dark grey clouds billow up from the island of Raasay. Portree has a nearby pharmacy that I haven't ransacked enough; but I did take some vitamin and mineral supplements that have been life savers.

I'm outside, making my way along the waterfront again. Black clouds leak across the sky like an ink stain. I'd like to get back to the farmhouse, before these rains.

Odd that I haven't seen one body, I think, as I walk away from Sea Breezes. They all got infected and wandered off, I assume, to collapse elsewhere in town, or be subsumed in packs of reivers that, lucky for me, haven't made it downtown today.

I walk along the wharf, back in the direction from whence I came. Beneath me is a sizable vessel, still roped to its piling and beached on the broken shore. It's worth a try, I think. If not food, I'll find tools. One time, I went down into a boat here and found a few fish on crushed ice in the hold. What a feast later! But that was winter…

I carefully climb a ladder down to the main dock, which is metallic and still intact. I walk down the pier and to a ramp that brings me right up to the deck height of the vessel. The vessel has rust and peeling paint on its hull, but I can make out *Rich's refuge.*

Soon, I'm on the deck, poking around. A lot of rust and frayed ropes and smashed crates; salt water sloshing about. A deeply malodorous whiff stops me in my tracks; that's not rotting food. It's worse. It's human. The odor is of death.

CHAPTER 10

I set my pack down, and begin to explore the boat's partially enclosed cabin. A captain's seat is empty; there's a sextant, a folded seafaring map, and a couple of empty beer bottles. A thermos.

The map is great and the thermos would be good but it's probably filled with mold...

I take the map and shove it into the side pocket of some cargo pants.

That stench is still pouring up from below. I consider cutting short the search, taking the smell as an obvious dark omen. But something draws me to continue giving the boat at least a cursory once-over. I've made the effort to get here. I can score more stuff.

The smell comes from the hold. I move the backpack down to the top of the entrance to the hold. It's too narrow to wear it as I descend. I have a yellow buff on my neck. I pull it up over my face. The ladder is metal and has narrow steps. I climb down into the hold, which has water sloshing about on the floor, and emits weak light through a small broken window.

I wince and look around. Plastic containers and other debris float in the flotsam that has begun to fill the hold. An unholy stink prevails.

The space is only about 20 feet by five. One wall is taken up by two bunk beds; the bottom one is partially submerged by the bilge waters. The top one has three people crammed into it, all clinging to each other, arms and legs akimbo, blankets pulled over their heads.

Dead, unless I'm dead wrong.

I take a deep breath, feel my heart race. The top of the bodies and blanket has a blood-stained envelope on it. To avoid the sloshing floor, I step on stacked cushions, reach over, and snatch the envelope away. One of the top blankets falls partly away.

A man lies on the bottom, as if he pulled the other two people on top of him. Right near his head and left hand is a pistol and a black bloodstain.

At the end of the hold, about 10 feet away, A locker stretches the width of the boat. I overwhelmingly feel like wretching; I turn my head away and gag. I can take the stench for maybe five more minutes. The envelope says, *The food is good.* I open it.

It contains a note, hastily scrawled in pen. It reads:

Whoever finds us, please take the food, if you need it, from the locker. God forgive me, please. I've killed my wife and son. Now I will do myself in. We've caught the forgetting. I was not going to let us go through that. I hope you are not sick. I hope I will not go to Hell. For God knows what I have done and let happen.

Whoever you are God Bless you and good luck,
Richard

"It's not your fault, Richard," I say out loud. "Not your fault."

I place the note back in the envelope and put it back where I found it. I carefully make my way along the lower bunk to the locker at the end of the hold, averting my eyes from the pile of stinking, embracing bodies.

Flip the locker lid; some more flotation cushions, a fire extinguisher, a dead utility flashlight.

Why didn't he flee? I think. Before they were sick? In the boat? It was winter, there was a storm, no fuel, no time. He must have had a good reason.

The right-hand section of the locker is stacked with cellophane-wrapped filets. To one side is shoved a box of Walker Shortbread. It says *Gluten-free* on the cover. *Who gives a shit,* I mutter, tearing open the box and eating down the biscuits.

I can hear my ravenous chewing, as if I'm watching someone else, with a glare of disapproval, gluttonously devour a box. I eat half the box, remove the inner lining containing the rest of the biscuits, and shove them into the pants side pocket. Food for the walk home.

The filets are the real score–*quality protein and Omega 3*– if I'm lucky and they've not gone rancid. I seize one off the top, hoping, praying that they are still edible. I peel off the wrapper and smell; fishy but fine. The fish is nicely filleted with streaks of black and white. He grilled and heavily salted them; smart. Brilliant, Richard. They must have been there for weeks.

I take a big bite from the one I peeled. Chewy, delectable, salty, I eat half of it, then place it back on the pile.

In an arduous process that seems longer than it takes, I carry four wrapped filets at a time to my backpack, across the bunks, avoiding sloshing my shoes in the water, or touching the reeking bodies. I carefully layer the fish within the small space left on top of the pack.

The air is amazingly clean and breezy above deck. I stand and take deep breaths and gag the rest of the reek out of me. I put the backpack back on, feeling revived and joyful from the "snacks" I've scavenged: Irn Bru, pickles, Walkers shortbread, and weeks old salted fish. More water. I've got two hours back to the farmhouse, given the weight on my back.

I hoist the pack and tighten the straps. Then I hear a sound.

Muffled voices from afar, over the rooftops, beyond the wharf. It reminds me of a protest, hearing a chant from a crowd of people. I wait a moment; no, I hear it again. Carried on the wind, up a hill that goes down from the edge of town to the Portree waterfront. But it couldn't; couldn't be human. I unhitch the pack and set it down.

I go over to the mast and start climbing. It has a narrow ladder. The mast is quite high, almost as high as the boat is long. Climbing is slippery, awkward in boots. Carefully I make my way to the top. The view clears the roofs directly in front of me.

A swarm of people march down the street and heads towards the wharf.

CHAPTER 11

They move in no orderly fashion, an ant-like swarm. If one falls, they're trampled and absorbed. The mass rolls along. A sound like a muttered protest rises into the wind. But they are not *people!* They *can't* be reivers, I think.

I've never seen more than a dozen. This must be 500, at least. Never before have I witnessed "group feeding" like this. They will lay waste to the landscape; the caloric demand is exponential. I feel utter horror.

They keep attaching new members, like metal slivers are sucked to a magnet. They are one organism, indivisible, I have no defense against that.

Down the mast, onto the deck, snatch the pack, off the deck, on the ramp. Back up to the street; too late! I hear their feet descending the hill above, a pattering and crunching like a giant pack of rats. Back down the ramp; boats along the wharf. I can't go back down into that reeking hold! Amongst the flotsam and wreckage is a wooden dingy, it has survived by its lightness and tendency to bob on top of the waves and the tide.

I wade out, up to my thighs, the muttering coming in like weather, loud like madness, the backpack like a load of lead on my back. I unwind the rope tie, toss the cricket bat into the dingy, unhitch the backpack, dump that in, one leg up; don't tip over the dingy!

I hop, roll, and I'm in the dingy, righting myself and paddling like mad in the shallows, the cricket bat my only oar.

The hand axe, strapped on the pack's side. I free that and place it on the dinghy floor.

The vanguard of this ghastly army has reached the street next to the wharf. The crowded faces, grimy with insane grimaces and lidless stares, line up along the waterfront. Then, as if in response to a silent command, they pour down the ramp to the waterside.

Driven by blind instinct and insatiable lust, they pile into the water like lemmings. Hundreds of arms thwacking the surface, tiny heads above the chop and the thrashing water. Stroke…stroke…stroke…frantically I dip the "oar" into the foamy loch.

Soon I'm beyond the shallows and out into the harbor, grimly dipping my cricket-bat oar with exhausted shoulders that burn with pain. I decide not to look behind me; the island of Raasay fills the horizon. I'll paddle all the way if I have to. I'm paddling for life.

The reivers sort themselves into a Vee shape, as the frenzied conglomerate begins to break up. I pause my frantic rowing and look behind. One creature plows ahead and is within ten yards. This maniac can really swim!

*Emma never gives up! I will not lose my hard-earned provisions to them! I will fight to the end…*he's caught the

42

dinghy; a bald pate covered with angry veins, mad, unblinking eyes. I swivel in my seat, take aim, and brain the bald pate with the cricket bat. Full on hit. He goes down for good. Davey Jones' Locker.

Another reiver grips the edge of the dinghy and starts to rock it; then another. I smack at both their hands, and when that doesn't work, I grab the small axe and have at their fingers, which quickly separate from their sockets. Blood spurts as the two fall back into the sea water, fingers and a part of a hand still weakly fastened to the gunwale.

I've got blood all over my forearm; I use the buff to wipe it all off.

I pick up the cricket bat and smash one more head that has swum close. This was the first woman I've really clobbered. She drifts back serenely as if baptized, and submerges. I keep having to remind myself; there are no genders among this doomed brood, in the conventional sense, or any remaining signs of humanity. Hearts beat in a soulless corpus made up only of ill, poisoned instinct.

Onwards I paddle, exhausted triumph, the dinghy only partly in need of baling.

Not designed for water, the reivers have finally lost their advantage. They summarily drown, or, unhitched from the massive raft of the sick, just as on land, they drift and swim away confused, brain dead, destined to die in the deep waters or collapse onshore.

So many have died in the cold waters. I don't feel like a mighty warrior. They feel like mercy deaths, a form of euthanasia.

Emma lives on for another day.

I make for the middle of the loch. The worst is over. I breath easier, but I'm exhausted.

Fog drifts in. I have only a vague sense of being in the middle of the harbor. Wind, briny and cool, induces uncontrollable shivering, even though I'm covered in sweat from the life-saving exertions. I cry for minutes on end, in rhythm with my oar, the sobs carrying across the water like a melancholy poem.

Against my will, I lay back against the backpack and drift off.

CHAPTER 12

I come to in the dark. I'd let the dinghy drift. I'm headed out to sea, but I've got no flashlight or any other light source.

Clouds like shredded black velvet cloak the stars. A salty breeze blows over the gunwale. A feverish dread rises. I seize the backpack for food, finishing the shortbread, guzzling an Irn Bru, devouring the half piece of salmon.

The calories clear my head. The pocket compass; I remember I have it.

I'm paddling west, which is to my left, unless I'm completely turned around. Which I could be since I've drifted on dark waters. After an excess of rummaging, I fish the compass out of a side-pocket of the backpack. I hold it under my nose; the arrow bobs about loosely until it settles on a northwesterly reading. Northwest would take me out to open ocean, which will swallow me up like Jonah.

I want due west. That will take me back to the Skye

shoreline, from where I can trudge to the farmhouse. If I've already drifted past the northern, outmost Skye coastline, tacking west will maroon me in the open ocean, drifting towards Iceland.

The clouds shift, leaving moonlight that glistens on the black water. Through a grainy evening mist, I spot the ghostly forms of rocks and trees. I rejoice when I hear water slapping on the rocky shore. But hopefully, I'm not on Raasay, because that means I'll have to paddle across the harbor again.

Just ahead of the prow is an inhospitable, rocky coast. I paddle slowly, looking for a place to beach. I finally spot a small cove, with seawater washing back and forth over flatter rocks. I paddle into this cove; the prow of the dinghy knocks gently on rocks. Thank God for this seaworthy boat, I think, for sparing me. It's been years since I've been to church but…thanks be to God.

I wonder how much time to sun-up. I climb out of the bow of the boat, unsteadily standing on rocks with my shoes in cold, knee-deep water. I tie around my waist the line to the dinghy; I'm not ready to set this craft adrift. I yank the backpack off the boat, pull my sore arms through the straps, then back off slowly.

I have to find a place to tie up the dinghy. I use a thick root from a coastal tree.

The dinghy secured, I pause and look around. No signs of predatory life, only the sea water lapping on-shore and the soft knocking of the dinghy in its mooring. I move heavily up and over rocks and pull on roots to aid my progress, until I'm finally on solid shoreline.

I set the backpack down. There's a path along the coast. I know where I am now. A gratefulness, a reassurance, washes through me. I stop shivering. I'm able to pull a few extra shirt

46

layers from the pack, don them, and go into some bushes to lie down. *I really need a fire,* I think, *a warm fire would be really nice*...is my last thought when I fall asleep.

I wake up with a start. It's still dark. Those faces in the water, bleary, mutant demons from the deep, gripping the gunwales, the dead, severed fingers like fat worms, lingered in my dream.

Still, I feel refreshed, but stiff and sore. I stand, stretch, and when I look out onto the horizon, east beyond Portree, I see a shaft of light, moving along horizontally in the darkness. Miles away.

The only lights I've seen, in 540 days, are from structure fires in Edinburgh and Portree and other places. The random burning vehicle, abandoned by the side of the road. I stare at this light. It's not an illusion. It's the first machine light, unless my eyes deceive me, that I've witnessed in years.

I watch the wavering beam till it fades for good.

It's a fluke, or it's a sign of mankind. I juggle the possibilities. You see, I don't even spot any aircraft these days. There would have been planes over the U.K. if pockets of military or government still existed. Helicopters, Air Force jets, light surveillance aircraft, not even a drone for Chrissakes. There's been nothing.

The sun rises, lighting up the coastline. I hike along it toward the stone farmhouse. Tall, dark green headlands loom, like tidal waves frozen in time. When it brightens, I glance at my forearms, blood-stained, bruised, and pocked with recently formed scabs. You never notice your wounds until after the skirmish.

I have a wave of paranoia about infection, even though I've shown considerable resistance to the pathogen. I have no idea what the mechanism of resistance might be; I have my theories, that's all. There are no guarantees, however, that I remain H7N11 free. And here I've splattered reiver blood all over me.

I have to disinfect the wounds; I walk faster. Coastal path to dirt road and up the lush grass paths and down a swale, to the familiar pasture. This field fronts the stone farmhouse, tucked away in vegetation and basking in the sunlight.

Hope wells up through the fog of exhaustion, the sun hot and high in the sky. A tight copse of woods, three shades of green, gleaming fields of buttercups and gorse. Finally, choked by its own hedges, the farmhouse stands like a heroic, bucolic symbol. Of what? Surviving civilization.

Down goes the pack, leant against a rock I'm familiar with. I just can't lug it anymore. My legs scream for rest. I head for the farmhouse, push open the door to the musty interior, weakly lit by shafts of light through half-shuttered windows. My makeshift kitchen. Nothing's been ransacked, neither my meagre food nor belongings.

The wooden table with the crumbs of my last meal. The thick-legged chair scraped to the side, my dram cup, the warm, non-electrified fridge where I store my provisions.

I rush forward, snap open a cabinet above the sink, and seize a bottle of propylene glycol. Uncap it, pour it on my bruised forearms and hands. The sting throbs just beneath the skin.

Through the open door, out across the pasture, I kneel at the small stream and dip both forearms and watch the flow clean off the bloodstains. It's not my blood, I remind myself.

Back at the farmhouse, I take the Laphroig 15-Year-Old and pour a dram. The first sip is miraculous, followed by more of a quaff. I wipe my mouth with the back of my hand. The bloody buff lies on the wooden table before me, like a strawberry-streaked serviette.

The easiest way to virtue is to stop drinking. I don't see the point of self-denial, at present. I consider myself damn lucky to have Laphroig 15, and pour myself another. One more bottle, cherished, rests in the wooden cabinet.

If you have a proper, high-powered microscope, that bloody buff contains everything you need for analyzing the pathogen that's brought humanity to its knees. Everyone, that is, but Emma Wallace Blair, who still stands strong.

Another sip, strong one. We just didn't...have...enough...time. Time...to at least settle on an etiology. The pandemic came on too strong.

Why hasn't it affected me?

CHAPTER 13: FALL, 2026

Leaving Will in bed, I left for the W.H.O. office where I worked. I already had an urgent text message from my supervisor, a research scientist. "8:30 meeting on the outbreak. all must attend," it said.

The understatement was almost ludicrous.

I parked my bicycle and went to a crowded, nervous conference room where a staff scientist stood ready to present, with a few slides. There was a murmur and a somber mood in the room, a prevailing sense of alarm and dread.

Not even when Ebola briefly made it to the U.S., did I sense this. The presentation began, the gist being: A novel, highly virulent, highly transmissible strain of Influenza A had infected the population. Patient X was thought to be in Denver, originating from a lab that had a Pentagon contract. This gave rise already to rumors that a bioweapon had been released to the wild by mistake. But I sensed, cover-ups were quickly in the works.

Starting in Denver, millions in the U.S. and abroad had been infected. *No shit Sherlock*, was the first thought that came to mind. *But what about efforts on antivirals and antitoxins? What's happening in that regard?* It appeared far too late for quarantines.

The virus was classified officially as: A/Denver/1/2026 (H7N11). Meaning, that it was the first strain of H7N11 originating this year in Denver. "H" and "N" are proteins that inhabit the surface of Influenza A viruses. The H7N11 pathogen aggressively attacks the Central Nervous System, causing rapidly worsening dementia-like symptoms and a "crowding" or "herding" behavior among groups of the infected, never seen before among ill humans.

"New York City has a widespread outbreak of H7N11," he said. "There is already a state of emergency." A hush fell over the room, then hands shot up among the scientists. I checked my messages; no texts from Will. I told him to text me how he was feeling.

"Do any antiviral meds work on it?" someone shouted.

"None, yet. Obviously, the tests are preliminary."

"Are labs free to test drugs on infected humans?"

A pause, then "They gave us the green light to find a solution…we haven't found animals that can be infected to test, anyways, except maybe elk or deer. So it will be on infected humans."

"Is there a fatality rate, or is it too early to tell?" another asked, calmly from the front row.

"There's no etiology for this disease yet…we're only in the first 48 hours. We don't have a patient who's been infected and presented with symptoms, then recovered. It's too early for that; there have been deaths, however. Many. If you're asking, the fatality rate, at this stage, is 100 percent."

A bunch of people yelled out questions, talking over each other. Others shouted for order, then the presenter said, "Most of the infected in New York are in the streets. They're right outside this building. Surely you've seen that with your own eyes!"

"What's the source of the virus?" I yelled out, finally getting my voice heard. "Where was the initial outbreak?"

"The research lab in Denver. This is unsubstantiated background but…it seems the ancient remains of an infected elk were exposed by extensive melting permafrost in Canada. The carcass was brought to a lab in Denver. The elk hosted the pathogen, a xenophobe…it jumped to a researcher, who spread it among humans…"

"That's bullshit!" someone yelled out. "It was a bioweapon that got out!"

The man standing upfront grimaced, then rejoined, "Regardless of the source, we're in deep trouble here. There are staff members who are infected; they never made it to work. An unprecedented situation is unfolding…We need to get to work!"

"Someone's gonna pay for this," the same guy, who'd gone from staffer to heckler, yelled back, then others turned to him, "Shut up!"

"Any more questions?"

"Has work begun yet on vaccines?"

"Of course, but as you know these things take time. An element we don't have right now is time…we have to give a press conference in 15 minutes. We have to avoid a panic."

Then he looked at the wall and spoke. "There's already a panic. I saw a march, a herd of them, going down First Avenue, on my way over here…"

Them. Already dehumanized. Probably appropriate.

"What do we do now?" someone said from the middle of the room, somewhat weakly.

"We get to work. We have samples, from infected blood. We start testing existing antivirals. It's not rocket science; we know it's a virus, H7N11. Tests are already on-going. We're communicating with offices in Geneva, Paris, Berlin, Moscow, Oslo..."

"Are there outbreaks then, in Europe?" I cried out.

"Yes, I'm afraid...wherever airlines go from Denver and connect from Denver, there are outbreaks of this H7N11."

"Are there any links with the deer wasting disease?" someone else asked.

"That's a bacteria, not a virus. We're looking into it, though, everything." Deer wasting disease was caused by eating infected meat. The disease attacked the brain, transferred to humans, and was similar to Mad Cow Disease.

"I have to go...the press conference..."

Another W.H.O. higher-up sitting at the lectern said, "Everyone check on your family members, be safe, and God protect you..."

"What do we tell them, our families?" someone asked mordantly.

A pause, then, "Tell them to avoid other people, even you, and flee to the countryside. Find a place where they can be alone, beyond crowds. Or if they don't have a place to go, sit tight...listen to the radio...wait for news from officials...that's all I can say. Good luck."

I'd been around Will; he probably had it. If I was infected, I'd know it now. I had to check on him though, soon.

"How soon when you're infected do symptoms present?" I yelled out.

The man was already pacing, gathering his papers, heading out the exit.

"As far as we know, instantaneously. We're distributing a fact sheet. Get to your labs! God speed!"

CHAPTER 14

Thinking of Will, and the low probability I could possibly honker down in a lab and be productive, I left the office building. I ran across a courtyard to where I had locked my bicycle.

Sirens shrieked, helicopters hovered overhead, panicked people ran in every direction. I saw a teacher herding terrified children. My first instinct was to help her. They were running into the open door of a neighboring building, she got them all in there. Then she suddenly stopped, the door closed behind the last child, and she slumped against a pole that held up an awning, staring vacantly at the sky.

I felt like I was watching the virus spread and present with symptoms, among hundreds, in real time. But it was impossible to distinguish the merely panicked from the sick and still ambulatory.

I mounted my bike and booked out of there, through the

chaos and the gridlocked traffic, mainly abandoned vehicles now. Traffic had ground to a halt. The helicopters had left, as if merely reporting and detached from the upheaval below.

The NYPD squad cars were empty, doors left open, blue lights uselessly activated. I saw a crowd of people, mindlessly pouring down the avenue. It contained NYFD men, but with their hats and coats doffed and lost. There was a din; screaming, sirens, car horns.

I peddled madly back toward Chelsea, taking Ninth Avenue south and stopping for nothing. I parked the bike in front of our building, leaned it against a tree, sprinted up the steps, unlocked the front door.

A black pool of blood stained the foyer. No one around. I ran up the four flights, burst through our door, screamed "Will!"

Silence. I went into the bedroom, wadded up pillows and sheets, an open window. I rushed over to the window, I thought I saw him on Seventh Avenue with an aimless group of possibly infected citizens. I screamed "Will!" again, "It's Emma!" Like a mother who sees her lost child everywhere.

Whomever I may have mistook for Will, another lanky 30 y.o. with black bushy hair and a T-shirt, blended into the roaming mob. I yelled again, some of them looked up at me.

Their contorted faces expressed a painful rictus. The group lurched in one direction or another without purpose, responding to crude stimuli, like flies banging against a screen.

I leaned out the window calling after them…"Will!" They disappeared around a corner. Others simply collapsed in the gutter and lay there in the fetal position, like they'd fainted and died.

A berry on a bush can grow and ripen in one day. A thousand leaves on a tree can change color; an embryo can

56

grow its legs. Mother Nature works in a mysterious, complex, heartless fashion.

In our hyper-connected world, an acutely transmissible virus spreads to a billion people in 24 hours. Three billion in 72 hours. And so on…and on and on…

All except me.

CHAPTER 15

I had another text on my phone, from my friend Klara. Do I want a ride to Canada? Then I got a text from W.H.O. that said two chartered flights were leaving from J.F.K. to Geneva, Switzerland and Edinburgh, Scotland in two hours.

If I got there in time, there's a seat for me. But they weren't going to wait. Then the battery went dead; I wasn't going to try to recharge it.

In five minutes the electricity went out in my apartment. I quickly gathered a few more things into my backpack.

I could ride a bike to J.F.K., without delays like closed bridges, in slightly less that time. About an hour and a half.

I could ride through the East Village, then onto the Williamsburg Bridge...as long as it hasn't been shut down. The first thing they do is close the bridges from the city, in a last-ditch attempt to contain an outbreak.

In the movies, Manhattan is then nuked. But surely, they

*have a more sophisticated emergency plan? Maybe they've
exhausted their protocols, there is no Plan C or D? This is
Zero Hour?*

Back outside, onto my bike, through the Village, past
Washington Square Park. Burning buildings, cars afire. Emma
against the clock. Pack on my back. I see a policeman shooting
aggressive, infected victims. One, two collapse into contorted
positions onto the pavement. Spurt blood. He holsters his gun
and runs chaotically through the park.

I'm on East 4th, zig-zagging idled cars and collapsed
people, onto the sidewalk. My head down, I bike back onto the
street. I make Delancey Street. I think of *What ifs?* I miss the
plane, Manhattan is not where I want to be. I'm on the
Williamsburg bridge, pressing on the pedals with all my
strength, sweat flowing down my face, wind in my hair.

Both lanes are gridlocked, but nothing's moving, vehicles
left empty, I have the space to ride.

I watch a group of people, one by one, climb up onto the
railing, as automatic as lemmings, then plummet to the sea-
blue East River below. They make little splashes, like bags of
junk thrown off the bridge.

A fleet of fighter jets roar overhead. I've made the Queens
side of the bridge. I enter a highway, go north, follow the JFK
Airport signs. Wind; crunching of wheels on roadside gravel.
The highway is no longer used by speeding cars, there are the
usual wrecks and empty, oddly idling NYPD squad cars.

Anyone in their right mind, and with a tank of gas, I
thought, had long ago fled the Metro area.

Then I witnessed a massive air strike about a half mile
away, in the direction I was headed. It was like watching a
mountain erupt, but from a thrilling, marginally safe distance.

The jets had dropped bombs on residential neighborhoods,

but a relentless survival instinct I wasn't aware of before, a tunnel vision, hurled these thoughts and the horror of the world around me coming apart at the seams, out of my mind. It focused me only on the grinding pedals and turning wheels and not getting lost.

An airliner is leaving…

My primary fear, flat tires. I knew the tires were low. I'd certainly ground through some splintered glass in the breakdown lanes along the way. Yet they got me, miraculously, to J.F.K. Terminal 1. I arrive covered in sweat, trembling, my throat parched and raw, half in tears. I abandoned the bicycle at the curb, reluctantly, as if it was a child.

I ran into the terminal, toting my meagre things; clothes, sunglasses, dead phone, a hair brush. Bare medical essentials, including my CBD oil.

Crowds holding onto a restrained panic, many wearing masks. Heavily armed military people waved people on, only after shining flashlights in faces and shouting basic commands. *Name, destination, I.D.!* An infected person couldn't handle that.

I rushed forward with my pack, ignoring everyone and everything, as if in a tunnel. The normal security and check-in procedures had been replaced by ad hoc emergency-based chaos; names on lists and restless lines of people pressing forward at the departure gates.

The flight left the tarmac bound for Edinburgh not fifteen minutes after my terminal arrival. I slumped into a seat at the back of the crowded plane. I thought of Will and my other friends. I quietly sobbed, exhausted, hand on my face, wondering why I hadn't been killed on the way, why I wasn't infected.

It didn't feel like a gift for which I should be grateful. It felt

60

like raw, elemental survival. I was one among the few.

CHAPTER 16: SPRING, 2028

Daylight through the farmhouse window. I think of the light I saw in the distance at night. A moving beam piercing the darkness. I lie in bed re-imagining it, watching the steadily moving beam across this wooden ceiling. That was no fluke. Somehow, I need to investigate the phenomena.

I throw the heavy blanket off, like it's made of chainmail. The front door is latched. I get up, pad across the wooden floor barefoot. I make a stove fire and heat the water up. I hear the wind through the trees, like a giant comb gently traversing soft hair, as I sit cross-legged and watch the water come to a boil.

I take the tea outside. There are clouds, but shafts of sunlight leak over the long grass and the fiercely yellow buttercups. I walk barefoot around the grounds, casually for once, feeling a profound relief coming over me, like an intoxicating drug, approaching contentment.

I gaze out over the landscape, nothing moving. A few

blackbirds dart across the sky, in and out of trees. Rolling swards of green hillsides, the dun mountains and a violet hint of the loch on the horizon.

I saw the lights last night due east, towards northern Scotland. They had to have been generated on the mainland across the waters from Skye, unless I'd dreamt them.

I go inside to sate my growling stomach. Cook salmon on the oven fire, a big scoop of oats mashed with potatoes and plopped on a ceramic plate. I scrape away with my fork and knife, those being the only sounds, the metal touching the plate.

That seems mournful, makes me lonely, so I take out my pipe and play a pretty song, the *Highland Widow's Lament*. This lifts my spirits, for a time.

I take my time with breakfast, make another cup of tea, add a splash of whisky. If I had to leave here, what would I take? I think. It breaks my heart to even consider vacating the farmhouse. I've made it my home. I'll never find another like it, with its shelter, the stove, the food stores (running out…), the dishes and pots, the river.

But the reivers have discovered this countryside. I've had two epic close calls in a matter of days, for the first time in months.

I don't have reinforcements or enough weaponry, beyond my cricket bat and mini-axe, to defend this lovely house. Scrape some more, the last morsels off my plate. Bring the pipe to my mouth, the music and whisky making me merry in a weary, wistful way.

I play chords and songs until I tire of it. I put the pipe down.

I'll pack my medical kit, leftover food, the whisky, vodka, and water bottles; the cricket bat and my axe. A few other essentials like the remaining match-books and the vitamin and minerals bottle. It's frightening, the very thought of leaving my nest.

I'll watch the landscape for 24 to 48 hours, and if it's all quiet on the Western Front, then maybe I'm okay staying put. It's a reassuring thought. But I'm going to run out of provisions again, and any thought of battling reivers every time I have to go into Portree makes a strong argument against staying.

Skye might have played out for me. I plan to scavenge at the vacant, decaying Cullin Hills hotel one more time. They have a broad bay view. I can look for the phantom light.

All these ideas are cycling through my head, but the whisky and the music has slowed them down a bit, made them appear like rational choices, rather than scattered thoughts. Never stop planning, Emma. Always have a plan. It's one of the survival mantras I cling to.

The way out is to walk 'n ride to the Kyle of Lochalsh, which is an isthmus that connects to the mainland. There's a bridge across the water, then other small towns I can harvest supplies from.

The whisky has gone to my head quickly, not surprising given the recent ordeal. I clean up a bit. I put plates and utensils away on the same shelf, since I would never waste water on washing, then I go outside with two water jugs.

Before I go to the river, I look down into the gully where I'd rolled the bodies. The female is still there, curled up and stiff among the wet matted leaves.

But oddly, the male I'd clobbered is gone. He could only have wandered off a short ways, and then collapsed. Everything else in the woods and fields, as far as I can see, is quiet.

The river water is cold and filled with floating bits of

sediment, like sticks, leaves, and bark. Undoubtedly, the water could carry other poisons that I can't see. E coli from sheep dung washed into the river, for one. I have disinfectant pills from the pharmacy in Portree, but I'm running out of those. Maybe one of those towns across the bridge has a pharmacy I can plunder. They don't all carry those tablets, but I don't care about that.

The not caring was the whisky, and the way I'd learnt to focus on only elements I can control.

I return the filled water jugs to the farmhouse, disinfect some water, drink it, put some in the teapot. I fill a small pack, including the part-empty vodka bottle (for refilling…) in preparation for the Cullin Hills mission. Then I catch some more sleep.

I dreamt that I saw Will crying out for me from a fourth floor window in the city, "Emma! Come back!" and that it was me, not him, pressed amongst and borne down the avenue by the demented herd. I put my arms in the air, beseeching, reaching toward Will, but it's as if I'm borne away by a rip tide.

It will be dusk by the time I'd reach the vacant hotel, I think, clearing the cobwebs out of my head while sitting on the edge of the bed. But I don't mind scavenging under the cover of darkness.

CHAPTER 17

I take the narrow rocky trail that follows the coast. Across the bay is the island of Raasay. The trail falls steeply to turquoise, sunlit water. I can see clear to the barnacled rocks on the bottom, as though I'm in the tropics.

Instantaneous beauty is still a tonic to me. I crave it and seek it out, standing by the edge of the trail and staring down into the shafts of light piercing the rippled waters.

I know the trail ends at the Cullin Hills hotel, precisely 1.6 miles from the Portree wharf.

I slow down, stop, listen. Silence, so far…so good. Only small waves breaking on the rocks and the distant cry of seabirds. I wonder how many of the reivers drowned in their attack on me. I wonder if their bodies are washing up on shore now, I think brazenly and mildly vindictive. I feel like the victor, as well as the eternally pursued.

I reach a splintered, falling-over sign for the Cullin Hills

Hotel. The path forks here and one part climbs steeply up through sun-dappled woods. The sun is beginning to go down behind the headlands that tower above.

The path ends at a open lawn, a tangle of weeds and upended, rusted metal lounge furniture. I can still imagine, like recently departed ghosts, the imported French waiters in their formal outfits and the spoiled tourists sipping on their Champagne and nibbling duck and salmon pate, as sailboats gracefully tack along the waters below.

The windswept loch in the near distance seems devastatingly empty. Except for a few half-sunken boats near the shoreline, the rough waters give off an air of pre-civilization.

Up a flight of steps is a solid oak door to the hotel. It hangs limply on its one unbroken hinge. I walk up the steps, enter the hotel. I find a foyer littered with random debris and blown-in leaves, an oddly still tidy checkin desk, with a dead computer sitting on it. A bar and dining room are adjacent to the foyer.

Tables are overturned, once nice upholstered chairs are gutted and gouged, windows are cracked. Food and mud stains spatter a beige rug like spilled paint. But no reivers, or bodies. I move toward the kitchen in back.

A demolished bar sits next to the main dining room. Behind the bar I find a basket of custom printed matchbooks, showing an etching of the hotel. I shove all of them into my pockets.

Above the bar is a once cherished, now cracked glass case for premium Scotch. It still has a few intact bottles. I take a Glen Livet 25-year-old and stash it in my pack. I don't have room for more than one, but I'll be back, I promise myself.

Behind the bar, amongst other bottles on a wall of shelves, is a two-thirds empty bottle of Belvedere Vodka. Polish, a fine booze that in any other circumstance I wouldn't dare to use only for disinfectant.

What a waste, I think. Oh…the gross insults to culture, like misusing great sipping vodka, that we make while scavenging and surviving…

I take my old vodka bottle out of the pack and fill it nearly full with the rest of the Belvedere.

I go around back to the ruined, savaged kitchen. It looks like a pack of hungry dogs have tore through it. The cement floor is littered with old gnawed-on chicken and lamb bones, egg shells, broken bottles, and stained tin foil that once contained ready-made dinners.

I wonder if someone hung out here and survived for a while.

The room is dark, unlit. But I can see, in the dim light, shelves and stacked boxes and a stainless steel counter leaning against a wall.

I wrestle out of my backpack and set it down on the floor. I light a match from one of the newly found books and tip-toe through the broken glass and the stains and the garbage. I find the counter surface dusted with salt and wet flour. A finger has traced a word on the powdery surface: *purgatory*.

I wonder whether an uninfected person scrawled that message at some time in the recent past. Reivers don't write or communicate, unless they've fallen into that pit of awful self awareness just before the forgetting sets in. As in the note I found on the boat, among the bodies in Portree.

Purgatory. It rings true.

I take the pithy message personally, marooned as I am on one shore of the River Styx, doomed to be denied for an eternity the warmth of another person's touch.

It's a purgatory of loneliness, that's what it is. But I won't ruminate excessively. I've got my music, my booze, my poems, and my sunsets.

I break out of this dour reverie and search the shelf above.; Bingo! A two-pound bag of rice. I give it a shake, look inside the clear plastic for tell-tale signs of mold. None. I tote it over to the pack, stuff it in. I dream of stewing it up with lamb and blood and salt. If I ever find any lamb, poor things. That gets my stomach growling mightily.

I keep searching. There's a door along another wall. It scrapes on the grimy floor as I push it open to a dank storage room. It's cool and musty like a vault, with the air choked with a sulfurous taint of rotten eggs.

I light another match. A stack of cartons of broken eggs; the dried orange yokes ooze down the sides of the cardboard. Next to those, crates of spoiled fruit, covered in a mossy green mold. I rip off a piece of dry cardboard, set a match to it, and make a crude, short-lived torch. I wave it around.

Leaning in the corner is the pay-off, encased in Dijon-colored wax, a large untouched wheel of cheese. The Mother Lode! I take the small axe out of the backpack and lay into the wheel with a series of dry thunks. Soon I've carved out a triangle, which I shove into my mouth as if it's my last meal and I've never eaten great cheese.

Never have I taken such gluttonous mouthfuls of cheese alone, a fine cheddar this one. A cheese full of healthy fat.

Fat, I crave more of it. Gristle gnawed greasily off the bone, tablespoons dripping with olive oil, pounds of fatty cheese like this. I keep chewing and hacking away at the wheel. I can't get enough of fat in my diet. I can't lose any more weight or muscle. I've got to stay above eight stone. Gotta stay sinewy and strong, Emma. So eat fat. And protein, like fish. Fatty fish, salmon.

I flay sections of cheese off the wheel, wrap them in the

leftover paper from the salmon, and shove them in the backpack. When I store the last piece of cheese I can fit there, I chop off a couple more to shove into my pockets.

I lift the now 20-pound heavier backpack onto my shoulders. I pause. Outside the kitchen, I hear plodding, creaking footsteps on the floorboards. Doors closing. The shuffling of awkward feet.

CHAPTER 18

I hold my breath. The noises appear to be coming from the dining room. I brandish the small axe in my left hand. The storage-room door is open a crack. I peek into the kitchen, nothing. I make my way, again tip-toe. To the kitchen door, which I'd closed behind me. I gently grip the knob, as though it was a baby's head. I turn it, soundlessly; finesse the door open, and look out at the dining room and bar.

I see both rooms full of reivers scattered and slouching about.

They're like mannequins. One sits at the bar, a disheveled gray head, dressed in a raincoat, collar up, a former gentleman. His head's in his hands. Another stands frozen and mute by a table, as if lost in thought or admiring the distant mountains through the picture window.

I open the door wider. No one's noticed me, or much of anything. Two other reivers are on the floor, motionless, like mimes. One female on her back, arms flat at her side, staring at the ceiling, another man sits cross-legged with his head bowed, not a twitch from finger or eyelid.

I have problems with the pronouns here. To me, they might as well be "it," not her or him. The disease has robbed them of distinguishing human or gender features. They are floating, bipedal (sometimes) bodies, in a terminal process of forgetting and erasure, until they finally keel over.

When they "crowd" or "herd," they become something altogether different, a relentless wolf pack, but lacking any wolf-like guile, only implacably driven by poisoned biology to gratify a primitive appetite. At least as far as I've seen.

Over by the checkin/checkout table, a line of three reivers patiently waits, as if trying to recall exactly when and why they made a reservation here, or simply trying to relive the lost pleasure of arriving at a hotel, a joy now diseased and withered.

Two more men walk in circles aimlessly between the dining area and the bar. That's nine of them, not ensnared together, as in the predatory crowds. They're too divided up by space; there must be at least five close together, to re-animate the multi-cellular beast known as the herd.

I've got nowhere else to go, no back door to escape through. So I grip the axe tighter and make my way into the room. I walk slowly past the bar, backpack tight against my shoulders. The man slumped like a depressed barfly pays me no heed.

I keep going through the dining room, past the guy and gal on the floor. Then the reiver gazing lifelessly out the picture window turns his head, the eyes unblinking. I don't make eye contact. He freaks me out but stays where he is.

I can see the hotel's entrance door, left open about 10 yards away. A cursory glance to my left, to a room that extends the dining room, more spilled and wrecked furniture, and there's more of them. It looks like a library full of mimes that move robotically or stand stock still.

I glide past the checkin table; almost to my exit.

One of the men standing in line turns and approaches me. To my trained eye, he has an un-reiver like swiftness. Maybe he's different.

Hit him with the axe and start running…No, I can't run too fast with the backpack on…hold your horses…don't overreact…

"Do you know why you're here?" he asks, monotonously.

"No…yes…I'm a guest." When I move, he sticks out a hand to stop me.

"I'm trying to checkin. You're the lady…here." His voice is a chilling monotone. "I know you. What you're about," he says hauntingly. "You're not eating…"

I look down at the hand on my shoulder. The two others walk over and join him, shoulder to shoulder, gaping at me vacuously.

"Where did you come from?" I say nervously.

Don't ask them questions idiot!

"I don't know. Why did you ask?" Now angry. "That!" His voice goes up a pitch, with an infantile rage.

"Are you going to help?" he asks, eyes all twisted up with the question. I note he's lost traces of any Scottish accent. The voice is just creepy, uninflected words strung together.

"Are you going to help?" the other two at his shoulder repeat, slack jawed.

With the hand not holding the axe, I move his own hand off my shoulder, as gently as I can. He jerks his hand away and looks at it in disbelief, as if I'd given him an electric shock.

Then he starts crying; the two get up off the floor and approach as he sobs.

That'll make five, the beginning of a herd...

I notice others coming from the extended dining room, with the sound of the crying. So they're crowding; I've seen enough.

I head quickly to the door, but feel a hard tug, a clinging, on my backpack. Two, three hands reaching out and clutching at the material–they're beginning to coalesce into a crowd; five or six together, more joining. I can't move at the moment, now is the time to react.

I swing around and whack one of the arms with the axe. It bites deep into the forearm and blood spurts onto the floor and onto the laces of my shoes. As if it's an octopus ensnaring me, I keep chopping away at the arms, swiping the axe back and forth in an arc, like a knight swinging his heavy sword. I hear my own desperate grunts, and taste the salty tears.

I'm walking backwards now, brandishing the axe. A dirty hand gropes for my face. I swing the axe wide and its top-heavy weight gives it momentum and the axe blade strikes the hand at the wrist, taking the hand right off. It plops to the floor like something wet and objectionable that fell from the sky.

I'm at the door, through it, moving sluggishly with the weight of the backpack, down the steps, the blood streaked axe hanging by my side. I plod downhill through the weeds on the lawn, past the rusted furniture, onto the trail.

Just before I turn the corner, I look over my shoulder; they've exited the hotel en masse, as if ordered to evacuate. They head straight for me. Faster than I can go.

Black bulbous clouds roil over the island of Raasay on the horizon. Dusk quickly dims to night.

Still sobbing, I hear loud, hurried footsteps behind me. The backpack has to go, I decide, not desperately, but winging it. I loosen the belt, but before I can get it off, flailing hands grab onto it from behind. Suddenly I'm jerked off my feet and forced down onto the trail.

CHAPTER 19

I flail back with the axe and hit flesh and bone, but my grip is exhausted and the axe slips out of my hand. Up I go into the air, hoisted like some kind of pagan sacrifice. Ghastly faces gawk up at me: gap-toothed, sweating, eyes lidless and red-streaked. The backpack still hangs from my shoulders.

I cry out, "let me go!" in a voice frightened and fruitless. They don't feast and tear in small spaces. Not on a narrow trail. Not like here. Does this buy me some time? I think, struggling against their firm, grasping, and wet clutches.

I shake in mortal terror. I can't control it. They're taking me somewhere, for dismemberment, into another open area, like the Portree wharf and streets.

The herd carries me downhill towards the ramshackle waterfront. I'm hauled roughly over their heads like a side of beef, on its way to the roast. I now know what the still-breathing impala feels like, trembling in the jaws of the leopard. I can't pry myself loose from these demons, however much I fight and claw and scream.

At the core of my terror is the knowledge is that I'm alone, so alone, and that I'll be slaughtered alone.

We reach the end of the trail, large, stately trees opening up to the broken war zone of the old Portree neighborhoods. I pull my arms away from their greasy clutches and punch and inflict any damage on faces and necks I can, *never stop fighting!* Above is the darkening sky. Black clouds roil, with the color of wet soil.

Heavy raindrops fall. I hear the hiss of the storm on leaves. The rain drenches my cheeks and mixes with the tears. My blows discourage the weaker of the herd, who appear to fall away, but there's so many of them, a many-headed beast.

It crosses my mind, for the first time, that I could have kept some kind of cyanide pill or the equivalent, for just this circumstance, a fate worse than death. Is it bonafide survival gear, if part of that gear is designed to kill you? The very idea of it flouts everything I believe in.

I think of what this means for the human race, possibly extinguished for good by a final act of pandemic-driven mayhem. A virus that man all but brought upon himself, by melting the permafrost to release that elk-hosted spore (or even bioengineering the germ itself), then releasing H7N11 into its overcrowded hives of billions of humans.

A species that had already caused massive extinctions, plundered vital resources, and slaughtered millions of its own with mindless wars.

What a melancholy legacy, I think, to leave this rock spinning its lonely path through the frozen cosmos, with only these pathetic, diseased creatures to inhabit it.

I fight and twist and kick and punch. Their clutches only

tighten. I hear my own convulsive sobs, against the wind and the pelting rain.

Me mum had made me memorize a Psalm when I was a wee girl...I begin mumbling it in a girlish voice, carried along by many hands like a Pharaoh's corpse toward the Portree wharfs.

Have mercy on me, O God,
according to your unfailing love;
according to your great compassion
blot out my transgressions.
Wash away all my iniquity
and cleanse me from my sin. (Psalm 51)

We near a wide open concrete section of road. I'm turned nearly upside down. The blood rushes to my head. I watch the rain flooding down the dirty gutter.

I feel my arms slipping from their slimy grips, as though they're preparing to drop me. I yell and scream at the top of my lungs as they lower me to the ground, lusty newborn baby screams, but coming from a still robust 28-year-old. All the ghastly faces gape down at me, as though I've been born into a nightmare.

Still screaming as loud as I can, I'm suffocated by arms and hands pressing down. Then comes the accelerating roar of a gas-powered engine.

CHAPTER 20

The black cab and grille of an old pickup truck slams into the crowd of reivers. It sends three of them flying through the air, others are bludgeoned and flung aside to the pavement. The pickup goes into reverse, crashes into four more, dragging the bodies beneath the vehicle. I hear bones crunching, the revved up cough of the engine, a roar of thunder, the heavy patter of the pouring rain.

"Get in!" a man screams from a driver's seat through the open window. I stand up, throw my backpack into the open cargo area; then grasp the side of the trailer and vault into the bed, my exhausted arms and legs spasming with the effort.

Reverse again, thick tires grinding into gravel, then forward, acceleration, wind, rain in my face, a wondrous sensation of life and freedom.

It's only me and a couple of red petrol cans in the truck bed.

Through a window, I see the back of the driver's ginger hair. He turns and points to the side of the road when we've put about a mile and a half between us and the decimated crowd. Then he pulls the truck over, opens the driver door partway, and yells, "Get into the cab!" More of a cockney than Scottish accent.

I slowly climb down out of the back–everything hurts–then he pops the passenger door for me and I slide in.

I stare at him mutely; another surviving human being. I am speechless.

"The word is 'thank you'," he barks when I'm silent for a minute, accelerating back into the road.

"You're not…"

"No, I'm not sick…I'm not one of those bloody sods."

"Well, thank you…I can't thank you enough."

"No worries. Where've you been hiding lady?"

"A farmhouse outside of Portree."

"You've been in Skye…"

"For the past year. Alone." He raises his eyebrows, impressed. Then he nods into the bed of the truck.

"I was gettin' some more gas for my truck. Been fillin' those cans from a tank in the back of a warehouse in Portree. It's just me, you know, in this world. I heard your screams. It didn't sound like one of those bloody bastards."

So he's clearly lost any empathy for the infected…like me…us against them I suppose.

"They're not human, you know, anymore," he says by way of explanation. He's talking loudly, like a deaf person.

"I know…"

"So you been livin' in Skye." He gives me another look over. "How come you're not sick?"

"I could ask you the same thing. You don't have to scream

80

at me. I'm sitting right next to you."

"Sorry…I have this bad habit…of talking loud to meself, like a blithering idiot. I haven't seen a human," then he coughs…"person, in more than a year. Been livin' off canned soup and spam and oatmeal and seabirds eggs and anything I can scrape up. Usually not too hard to find food if you have a truck…been making my way around the Highlands."

"Where do you live? I mean, where've you been staying?"

"Kyle of Lochalsh, right now," he says in a more relaxed tone. "I sleep and get shelter inside the passenger coach of a train."

"A train?"

"Yeah, it makes a good home," he says gesturing pleasantly with his right hand, while keeping the other on the wheel, as if this was just another agreeable conversation between strangers.

"I sleep in the passenger compartments. Got many of the comforts of home. Then I drive the diesel electric engine; it's what we call a DVT, a driver's cab connected to a coach. I got it working fine," he says proudly. "I'm testing it…longer trip, you know…"

"You're driving a train? A working train?" I ask incredulously. My voice sounds hoarse and strained.

"Yeah," he says grinning, clearly pleased at this overdue recognition of his ingeniousness.

"Have you done it at night?"

"You bet…up and down a bit."

"So that's what I saw, at night, the light…But how…?"

"I used to work for ScotRail, Aberdeen line." Then he winks at me, as though there's always been something mischievously cool about the Aberdeen line. "My name's Terry Winslow…friends call me Terr…"

"Emma Blair…I'm from Scotland. I was working in New

York City, though."

He looks at her meaningfully. "Pretty rough over there, eh?"

"Yeah. I flew to Edinburgh…barely caught the plane. I'm a scientist."

"What kind of a scientist?"

"A researcher of pathogens and germs…I worked for the World Health Organization."

"You don't say? So what is this bloody sickness that's ruined the world, eh?" His light remark makes the pandemic seem like sour politics, as if they should just elect someone else to get everything back on track.

"Well…it's called H7N11. It's a long story…I can tell you later. I'm knackered right now, thirsty, and *famished*. The train doesn't have a shower, does it? They…slimed all over me. It's disgusting…*gross*," I wince, almost good-naturedly.

"No shower, and we don't have high tea, Champagne, and duck pate either," he says smiling.

I like Terr. Not only did he rescue me, but he seems to be a friendly bloke too, not too weird. A bit cheeky, likable. Not thinking he's going to get after me, is what I'm saying. And he has a train…

"Where we going, by the way?"

"Kyle of Lochalsh. I park the truck next to the train."

I sit looking out the window in silence, at the empty beauty of Skye, as if I was lifted from the clutches of the damned, and dropped into heaven.

The rain has let up. The clouds skid across the tops of the green hills. The slick road glistens beneath us.

I can't believe I'm having a normal conversation with an intact, reasonably healthy person. A man. One more U.K. survivor. I can only pinch myself.

82

CHAPTER 21

"By the way," I say. "You haven't run into any *females*, have you? I mean, uninfected ones. Or males…"

"None," he answers, with a note of regret. "Not since everything went bollocks to balls. No men…women…children…" He looks at me, then stares back at the road.

"Were you married?" I ask.

"Yuh. Maggie, and two kids, Wendy and Francis. 10 and 7."

"I'm sorry." He shrugs, scratches his chin thoughtfully.

"I don't think about it too much anymore. I mean of course I mourn my family, but I'm busy now. I've kept me-self busy. You know how it is, keeping meself fed, the truck and the train runnin'. Watching out for those daft bastards. It happened to everybody. It's not like I'm surrounded by other families that are alive. We had some good times…"

Then he fingers a picture that hangs from the rear-view mirror, a smiling woman and two playing kids at the beach. The snapshot-sized photo, hanging from a bracelet, swings back and forth.

"It's not like I cry into my cups every night…"

"I do…I mean…cry a lot."

"That's a lady thing, no disrespect intended. Your lot's better than blokes, at weeping, that is. We hold it inside, then we have a few…" He bends his elbow to lift an imaginary glass. "…And instead of weeping, we throw a few haymakers…weepin's probably better when you're feeling down. Makes more sense. You married?"

"No, I was engaged."

"Too bad. What happened to the bloke?"

"He got sick in New York. I lost him one day."

"Tch-tch, well…" He rubs his eyes with the bottom of his hands. "We got you out of Portree, at least. Infested with them vermin. What did you call 'em back there?"

"Reivers…" I say, with an almost bashful embarrassment. "It's just a name I made up…the marauding gangs."

"Reivers, you say? I'll stick with bloody buggering sodding bastards."

"…That's the bridge," he says, as though to change the subject, pointing ahead. The bridge goes across an isthmus, from Isle of Skye to the mainland. "I towed a car wreck off 'a it the other week. Otherwise, we couldn't get across."

He smiles widely, again, proud of his work. He gives me a rough reassurance. After all, I've only known him for about an hour, and haven't seen what he's like drunk yet. But my conclusion so far is…a remarkably capable man in these or any circumstances.

He's missing some teeth in the back, but otherwise, is good

company and not bad in looks. I really can see what Maggie saw in him. Poor Maggie; I've never been good at tamping down the empathy for an individual and steeling myself that way, in light of the billions that are dead or got infected.

What was that John Donne verse, *No man is an island*...I mourn for all of them.

Soon enough, not far from the other side of the bridge, in the darkness, I can make out a collection of buildings and a modern locomotive with an attached coach. It's unbelievable. I stare at this sliver of remaining civilization. An unfamiliar warmth washes through me, an emotion, long having gone stale, that feels vital once more.

CHAPTER 22

The train looks like a modern relic, like we've pulled up next to a railroad museum. At the same time, however, it feels like the future, if Terr hasn't exaggerated his ability to get the rig running south into the rest of Scotland.

We park the truck. I get out.

"The food's in the train," he says, gesturing to a set of steps leading up to the coach, where a sliding door is open. He seems to imply it's dinnertime, and that we are to be roommates.

Short of sleeping in the truck cab, which I'm in no mood to do, I resign myself to sharing the coach, which is sizable, with my newfound companion.

He helps me with my backpack. "What do you have in here?" he asks. "It's heavy as lead."

"I've got a bag of rice, lots of cheese, Scotch, vodka…" His eyes light up.

"You don't say…"

I answer his question before he verbalizes it.

"We can have some of the booze. God knows I need a drink. But first..." My pinched voice squeaks. I have a raging thirst. "Do you have any water?"

"Sure, yes." Once inside the coach, Winslow disappears into the driver's cab and emerges with a plastic jug of water. I take it greedily and begin guzzling, murmuring and exhaling with pleasure in between gulps.

"Where do you get this?"

"Many different places...some houses in town still have partially filled water tanks. I find full jugs here and there. A restaurant has a cistern. When it rains, I fill up."

"Clever. I'm afraid of not being able to find clean water. You know what they say: we live three weeks without food max; three days without water, three minutes without oxygen."

He pauses and drinks from the jug when I pass it to him. The jug comes down and he spits out his words.

"It would taste better mixed with Scotch. Water of life, you know."

"Don't I know it..." I pull the rice, cheese, vodka, and Scotch out of the backpack, set them on one of the dining tables in the coach. I'm wary that he'll want to get pissed. If he does, then I'll truly get to know him tonight. Whether he has any self-control.

"Where can I clean up?" I ask. "I feel gross."

"You can go down to the boat landing and dip into the loch. It's cold, not that cold. Here, I'll get you some soap, and a towel." He efficiently fetches both from the driver's cab again, and I go outside in the dark and find the landing not far away. Not too private, despite the evening. I'm understandably nervous and checking constantly over my shoulder.

But I splash water and soap all over my extremities and

face and shoulders and hair and pull up my pant legs and cleanse that area, finding all types of random bruises and scratches. Then I return to the coach, and before Terr can say anything, I've laid down in a booth and pulled a coat over my head and passed out in a stupor.

I have that stranger-in-a-strange-land impulse when I first wake, which can't be three hours later. I sit on the edge of the seat, in a dim light, thirsty again. I see Terr outside the window. He's a dot of light, a glowing end of a cigarette, which pauses at his face, then drops to his side.

The water jug rests on the table and I take another hit. I gather my wits and step outside into the cool air.

He lets go of the butt and stamps it out when he sees me.

"Bad habit..." he says. "I take it you slept."

"Did I."

"I had a little snack and drink, but thought I'd wait for you before I had the big meal. I cooked up some cheese and rice; put some spam in it. Makes a right tasty goo."

"How kind...I am *so* hungry."

On the way back to the passenger coach, he says, "I've been eating alone for over a year."

"Me too."

"I didn't want to do it again."

"I don't either."

"You'll have a Scotch?"

"Sure, I'll take it neat. A dram."

As he pours some of the Glenlivet in two glasses, I say, "You know I was thinking, if you have the gas, we could go back to my farmhouse. We could recover some valuable provisions."

"If you think it's worth it, I'll take your word."

We clink the glasses, I take a sip, filling my mouth with the smooth Scotch. Just then, sitting in the company of a real person, feeling the smooth liquor go down, warming me all over, feeling safe, for just this instant, I sense my old world has been restored.

We dig into the food, quietly at first, then he chit-chats, as if he's at the pub.

"Where'd you say you was from?"

"I didn't," I mumble between gluttonous bites. "Inverness, small town outside of it. You?"

"Farnborough, near London."

"So how'd you end up here?"

"Working for ScotRail when the SHTF up here. Stuck in the middle, if you will." He takes the last sip of his glass, then looks at it as if he was disappointed in it. I fill it a bit more for him.

"I drove the train to the end of the line, after I unhitched the other passenger coaches. Trying to contact my family members. Everybody sick, the stations all chaos and bodies laying about, some on the tracks. I thought of going back to London, then the situation, all gone to hell, made me stay, due to being just down to daily survival, with no planning ahead.

"The whole time, I'm waiting to get sick. Waiting…waiting…sure, I was knackered by the pandemic, and not feeling myself, down and depressed, feeling ill-like, but the forgetting never came. Tell me, how come not us?"

"I have a few theories, all worth testing." I sip the Scotch, think about H7N11 and its etiology. God knows I've had plenty of time to ponder it.

"We might have a protective allele."

"What the hell's that? I mean, not that I mind having it…"

I then went into a more detailed explanation, which also helped me think through matters.

CHAPTER 23

"You have genes in the nucleus of cells, which are no more than instructions, and your body makes proteins off of these instructions. Okay, you with me?"

"Sure," he says blankly.

"With me and you, possibly, these proteins are made in a different variation. It's a variation we inherited. At any rate, immune cells are made of protein, and maybe this variant genetic allele makes proteins that offer some protection against H7N11. Rare as this protective condition may be." I hold the amber Scotch glass up in the air, as if it contains a theory I admire.

"Hmm," he said, nodding as sagely as he could manage. "So maybe there's more of us."

"Possibly. Also, the immune system is tuned earlier in life. I had a bad bacterial sickness as a young girl. Almost killed me. Maybe my immune system learned from that infection, and somehow this helps me fight H7N11. Especially in its early stages. There are lots of examples of people who have only minor flu symptoms from pandemics."

I went on, feeling the theories evolving, broadening, because I was speaking them. "Of course, there's also the anti-viral foods you eat. I've always eaten a lot of garlic, unfortunately for my breath, and olive oil, every day. Both strong antivirals.

"When I have it, I drink elderberry juice. Then there's CBD oil. I only have a little left. When the pandemic struck, I was taking more than a gram and a half per day of CBD, for my moods. I get depressed and agitated at work sometimes, and it really helped. Damn the anti-depressants.

"But all those things in my diet probably helped. I'm thinking about the brain, too. H7N11 attacks the Central Nervous System. Something protected our brains, me and you. We were almost certainly exposed to this powerful, highly transmissible virus, but it couldn't infect us and cause disease…"

"What was in your diet, before the…" then I laugh, at the term, "TSHTF?"

"My diet was like it is now, I would just grab anything to eat, that was around, when I was hungry," he says with a faint guilt. "Sandwiches, eggs, steaks, fish n' chips, pizza. As for garlic though, and olive oil, spaghetti bolognese, lots of garlic, antipasti with oil…"

"Do you have an Italian parent?"

"No, I just like the food. And you mentioned the CBD; I smoked a lot of hooch. I was a real teahead. You know, I got hurt, working on the train engines, and I started smoking a lot of hooch for the pain. Almost every day. Continued to…"

"You don't say…" I respond thoughtfully. We're onto

91

something here. "There are cannabinoid receptors, all over the body, but particularly in the brain. What if this virus highjacks the receptor; that's how it takes over the brain, gains access. But what if the receptors are turned off, because they're already busy or chemically bound by THC in your hooch, or CBD."

I get up and pace the aisle between the seats. "What if it's a combination of factors...the proteins we inherit fight the virus at the infection site, and if the virus gets through, it's denied access to the brain, because the cannabinoid receptors there are already bound. Then the virus may fade out; it might not have much of a lifespan outside of the brain...it has nowhere to go, it's disposed of by the body...you never get sick..."

"But I don't have any pot left..."

"I have CBD. When was the last time you smoked?"

"About eight months ago. Have had the jitters since then, aches and pains...you know, I really depended on it. So I've been drinkin', when I can...Not proud of it, but that's the reality of my situation. Haven't had too many brushes at all with the daft bastards since then. Finding you was the most of them I've seen. To tell you the truth..."

We both resumed quietly eating the delectable mush. I had almost forgotten how starved I was.

He spoke between bites. I notice that the booze and our dinner together has made him wistful.

"...The reason I want to go to London is to visit me home, and score some more hooch. I figure it might be easy to find in the flats and hospitals because it's legal since 2021...it must just be lying around."

"Now there's more reason to go get it, if I'm right about the cannabinoid receptors...I need more CBD myself. So you're serious...that we can make London?"

"So far so good. I think we have enough fuel to make at least one trip. Of course, there's no direct track to London; we have to make our way north and east. To Inverness, Edinburgh, then London."

"When were you planning on going?"

"As soon as possible. Work on the train a bit more. Gather provisions, including water, for the trip."

We have enough chat for one night. My belly is full, including of Scotch, and the horizon looks brighter than it has in months.

I look at Terr. He gets up and makes his way wearily to the front of the cab, where there's a passenger booth with some cushions piled up in the corner. I take it he's ready to pass out. He looks back at me once.

"I lock the door from the inside. Do you mind? I do it for safety…at night."

"I don't mind." I move over to the booth where I'd previously napped. For once, I wish I wasn't a cute lass. Even though at the moment I must smell and look gross, compared with my appearance say, when Will and I met. I lay back against the backpack, then I notice him standing beside my booth. He looks almost shy.

"Here's a pillow for you," he says, handing me one of the cushions, then he turns and shuffles away. I stick it under my head and before I know it, sleep comes over me instantly, like tumbling headlong into a deep dark cavern.

CHAPTER 24

It's painful to go back to the farmhouse, knowing that the visit is the last I'll see of my former refuge. But the car trip goes without a hitch. Gladly, there are few signs of reivers. We only saw a few bodies slumped by the side of the road, collapsed in the fields. I'd see a boot sticking up in the air, the sleeve of a coat just visible above a clump of weed grasses.

Winslow had a half full tank of gas. He wouldn't have to think of this much longer, because once we leave by train, the truck stays behind. I get the sense he's just as sentimental about the truck as I am about the farmhouse.

My memories of living there alone are also tainted by visions of the dark and lonely nights, rain and wind beating against the locked windows and doors, sleeping only fitfully and wondering what I was going to wake up to.

I still tremble inside, pondering how close I came to a gruesome end. It's a post-traumatic agitation, which I cope with by sitting in the sunshine that bathes the Kyle of Lochalsh, caressed by a gentle breeze, as well as sipping a wee dram at night. I chat away with Terr My Hair.

Playing my pipe, while he strikes a kind of rough drum rhythm on an overturned utility pail.

That's my nickname for him, Terr My Hair, partly because he's losing his hair (a stress response to our predicament). Mr. Winslow doesn't mind it; he's a fellow that likes a good joke, a laugh. Even at his expense.

Laughter is the cure for loneliness, among other things, like love. We both realize that we're not alone anymore.

We're not at the farmhouse two hours, leaving with all the leftover oats and rice, two dozen jugs of water from the river, and disinfectant tablets. We took all the leftover Scotch and vodka, numerous utensils, such as fry pans and pots. The salmon I salvaged from that boat. Blankets and pillows. We just about filled the back of his truck, even taking back my trusty cricket bat, the one with the seven notches in it.

We return to the Kyle, unload our booty. It's easy to drive around the narrow roads when no one is on them. Everything goes into the train, which I embrace as a new home. A home on wheels, which makes it all the more warm and reassuring. We'll be moving soon, northeast towards Inverness.

For the first time, my new accommodations give me the sense of living for more than just the next hour.

I find Terr leaning against a piling on a pier that juts into Loch Alsh, with a Scotland rail map unfolded in his lap. He takes a small wet towel and furiously rubs some black grease off his hands. He's been poking around the engine all morning.

The map shows the train routes through the north of the country. He traces the planned route with his finger, while describing it to me, breathlessly and hoarsely.

95

"We don't spend time in Inverness. I don't want to stop there, if we don't have to. Hope we can just roll through the station. It shouldn't be a problem. There's only one way for a passenger coach to go in Inverness, and that's south toward Perth."

"What could stop us?"

"A train, blocking our passage. I think all the trains went south to Edinburgh and Glasgow though, when TSHTF."

"If we get stuck in Inverness, don't you think we can find another truck, and gas? Then we can drive down to London. It can't be more than 450 kilometers or so."

I'm all in on Terr's plan to make it to London, by hook or by crook. But at least the train gets us safely off the Isle of Skye, and onto the Scottish mainland.

Terr tosses me a look of wary hope, and I instantly regret introducing any uncertainty about running his cherished machine over the Scottish rails.

"I want to take *my* coach all the way to London. We can do it…I don't want to be marooned with the daft bastards in Inverness. All of our supplies are on it. We can live there. It's relatively safe."

"So we stick with our amazing train," I add with a forced buoyancy, feeling bad about expressing my fears. "I've got a strong feeling that Inverness won't be a problem."

My hand strays to the top of his calloused one, which lays on the map. He glances at my hand stiffly, as if wondering what to do with it. I draw it away, as if it had ventured onto unknown, faintly forbidden territory. Then he smiles, embarrassed. The map shows all of the U.K., including Scotland and the rail lines, looking like stitches along the countryside.

"Inverness to London is more like 900 kilometers," he

corrects me. "Ideally, we do it in a full, 24-hour day."

I creep closer, leaning my shoulder on his. This time, he doesn't shrink from me, as he traces his finger over Scotland's main lines.

"We go east to Inverness, in the north. Then we head south by way of Perth, where I have to transfer the coach to the Edinburgh-Aberdeen line."

"Do we go to Edinburgh?"

"We pass through there, yeah."

I immediately think of meeting Will, and what a joyful time we had. Strolling the old city's wide boulevards in the spring sun, drinking in cafes, hiking through the gorse in Holyrood Park. Watching the sunset on Calton Hill, Will in my arms. I hadn't known him for eight hours. Sadness washes through and paralyzes me. I swallow a stubborn lump in my throat.

I'm haunted by the good times, and a clawing guilt because I'm still alive. But I wish, that if he was infected, that he passed away. The alternative is that he lurches around as a reiver, and that wouldn't be Will anymore.

"Do you know Edinburgh?" Terr asks.

"Yeah, I know the city pretty well. I grew up in northern Scotland. I wouldn't want to go there now…"

"We roll through Edinburgh Waverley," Terr mumbles, as much to himself. "From there it's just aboo't a straight shot, through York to London. We could be in London in 24 hours, barring any troubles."

"We have the fuel?"

"The diesel, yeah. For one trip. One way baby." When he says that I think, *a one-way trip to hell,* from some dicey action movie. Our plan is so outrageous, I think, almost anything could go wrong. We begin the perilous journey in just a few hours.

CHAPTER 25

"We'll pull into London's King Cross, stop, resupply a bit, live outta the train. For starters," Terr says. Then he stares wistfully at the gleaming sky-blue siding of the railcar, its ScotRail decal as polished as if it was getting ready to receive a coach full of Glasgow commuters.

The train looks like a railcar converted to hip restaurant. I can't fathom it moving from these ruined, perilous parts to the mainland, then connecting to Perth, Edinburgh, and York. Somehow, Terr the wizard has the means and the will to make it happen.

We eat a portion of oats and salmon that I stir up into a mush, sitting outside as the sun sets over the dark green headlands across the water. With little cajoling, I convince Terr to delay our departure until daylight. Once inside the train, as though profoundly released from pressure, he collapses into the booth next to mine and starts snoring.

I'm too excited to sleep. I step outside and look at the stars for a while, for some reason, thinking of the still coherent victim and their "Purgatory" message, traced in powdered flour. I no longer feel like I'm in purgatory, but headed for a fresh locale and its welcome unknowns.

I pull a blanket over my head and finally drift off, for I don't know how long. Then I awaken to a soft brightening in the window. Terr is already gone, having moved to the driver's cab out front. I gaze out the window to my last view of Skye, the undulating, deepening greens and browns as the sun rises through a watery mist off Loch Alsh.

A loud pneumatic sigh, the metallic squeaking of wheels, then an abrupt and violent jerk through the floorboards. An attempt to move the rig forward. Black diesel smoke rises from the train belly, an acrid curtain outside my window. Moments of paranoia as I fear mechanical failure, and the demoralizing effect that would have on Terr.

This fear quickly dissipates. The train rolls forward, picks up speed. I feel young and naive, a joy coursing through me. This childlike simplicity of train travel, as if momentarily rediscovered.

I watch the battered, empty remains of homes and small, boxy factories, smashed windows and pealing billboards, shift past in the window. Again, no sign of reivers, not even a random body in a field or on a street.

The train picks up speed, faster than 40 miles per hour. The Kyle's Atlantic blue waters are behind me. We enter a arboreal forest, penetrated by shafts of bright sunlight. It's beautiful. I eagerly open the door that separates the passenger section from the driver's cab. Terr, sitting at the controls, glances back at me with an ear-to-ear grin.

"50 miles to Inverness," he says.

"Marvelous. Do you need anything? Some water or food? Coffee?"

"You mean this rig has a dining car? No, not yet. Ab'oot 900 kilometers of empty track will do me." Through the front window, I see the steel rails, stretched over a bed of white stones, flying under the wheels. I go back into the passenger carriage to tidy up, sensing through the floor the smooth vibrations of movement and progress.

We pass Loch Cluanie, flat and unruffled, mirroring the desolate brown mountains rising from its shoreline.

Within forty minutes of the beginning of our journey, we're motoring alongside the 20-mile-long stretch of Loch Ness, heading north toward Inverness.

I stare out at its dark blue waters as we pass a few of the "Nessie hotel" tourist traps, now broken and abandoned. A sign drifts by: Welcome to the Original Loch Ness Monster Visitor Centre.

I'm getting into this "survival tourism," with nothing much to do but gaze out the window at lush blue lakes and overgrown, thriving forests.

It's before we pass Loch Ness when I get a shock. A large ferry founders and lists near the end of the lake. Dozens of people scurry like ants from the sinking vessel, tipped up at the bow.

CHAPTER 26

"Stop! Slow down!" I yell toward the driver's cab as I run from window to window, trying to keep the listing boat in view. I can see it through the trees on the shoreline. A panicked crowd of people scrambling along the rails towards the bow. I see a black and white dog in the bow, barking at them.

I quickly unlatch the door between the driver's cab and the coach. Stick my head in.

"There's a sinking boat out there on Loch Ness, full of people!"

Terr pulls back on a lever and applies the break; the train slows to about 10 m.p.h. He looks back at me curtly.

"We can't do nothin' for 'em. You know that. It's a boat full of your reivers. Its sinking will be a blessing. I'm not stopping the train. We've got the momentum going!"

"There's a dog…"

"A what?"

"There's a doggie on the boat! We can't leave him!" I think he picks up on my stubbornness, my desperation.

"Dammit!" A metallic shriek. The train slows, crawls to a stop. Nothing but woods, the lake, a stretch of track and empty track bed ahead. Terr pushes himself up from the driver's cockpit, goes to the window. Gazes out. The ferry, through the sun-dappled fan of leaves, is at least 40 yards from shore; sinking and foundering but still inching forward, no one at the controls.

People crawl all over it like rats. Some leap and splash into the water.

We pull down the window. Faintly, I can hear incessant barking.

I run down the aisle to the exit door, unlatch it I step down from the bottom steps onto the bed of stones. Terr yells from behind: "Come back Emma! We've got to get to Inverness! You've lost your head!"

"Give me ten minutes! I promise!" Thick brush and roots and tree trunks lead down a hill toward the shore. I see the boat listing, hear random shouts and barking, amplified over the choppy waters. Now the vessel's stern sinks farther, the bow sticking up in the air, the dog barking frantically.

More passengers falter and topple into the water, which the wind has whipped into a dark purple chop.

I descend sideways, triggering little avalanches of sand and pebbles. The boat is a faux paddle wheel, which now hovers in the open air pathetically above its name, the Maggie Mae. It was clearly designed for the tourists and shutterbugs searching for Nessie the monster. I figure now it has maybe five minutes until finding its watery grave, taking down all infected souls with it.

I'm convinced they're all reivers, something to do with the

102

awkward, weakly mechanical motions, and the way they flop like wilted plants over the side. They're also moving robotically toward the dog, perched on the prow barking with steady, high-pitched yelps.

I cup my hands over my mouth: "C'mon boy! Jump!"

I reach the shoreline, jumping up and down and waving my arms. "Hey doggie, jump! C'mere boy!" Screaming, I get the dog's attention. Its staring at me; stops barking.

Curious, tail wagging slowly, giving my directions some consideration.

I hear Terr from above. "Emma, we gotta leave this alone. Let's go!" The dog looks at me across about 40 yards of water, ears cocked. One reiver gets very close. Then I hear a deafening, groaning sound of weak metal structures giving way. The vessel tips acutely onto its stern and sinks like a knife into warm butter, taking down all the reivers, and the dog.

"No!" I scream.

CHAPTER 27

I dive into the water, shoes on, everything. Terr bellows behind me: "Emma, Christ!"

Ahead, the dark water boils and whirlpools; more metallic groaning, then the bow disappears. My arms thrash towards where the bow was. I'm not leaving until I'm certain.

I'm still in good shape. I've always been a good swimmer.

The first 30 yards go by. An oily acrid odor floods my nostrils. I dive beneath the slick and paddle through murky water. Through the depths of the lake I sense the boat dreamily descending, like some kind of profound relic of worship.

Finally, I surface, sputtering and thrashing. I see Terr on the shoreline, vaguely waving his arms. He turns to leave.

I'm in a frantic breast stroke, nostrils burning with the hydrocarbon fumes. Scanning the surface, I spot a soaked, black furry head, a pair of wide open, hopeful eyes. The dog turns and paddles toward me, just the head with the wet ears plastered backwards, navigating through the water.

I cough uncontrollably then croak, "You made it!" The dog exhales and puffs out its wet cheeks, in a rhythmic, canine way, barely staying on the surface but making steady forward progress.

"You Huckleberry!" I declare, for no particular reason. The last 20 minutes have rendered me an emotional wreck.

She pulls up beside me, motoring along. I reach out, but she shrinks away cautiously. Underwater, the dull paddling claws scrape my arms. She turns, as if operated by a rudder.

I see no other heads above the water. Loch Ness is windswept and placid, having swallowed the boat whole and its doomed cargo, which may as well never have existed. The oily stench lies thickly in the sun.

"Towards shore!" I command. I'm reassured when the dog follows. Finally, my feet touch bottom. The soaked scraggly mutt swims up with weary, trusting eyes. I grab and hug her and begin sobbing, standing up to my waist in the water.

The point where the vessel sank ripples with a faint eddy. The oil slick drifts away on the wind-driven current, like a small continent.

We wade toward the shore and Terr is already trudging to the top of the rise, rushing back toward his beloved train.

The dog reaches shore, stands, violently shakes herself dry. She's a black and white mutt, skinny, weighing no more than 50 pounds. A shiver goes through her, then she obediently sits down and aims a thoughtful look in my direction.

"Huckleberry," I say. "You are certainly not that." I check for dog tags and a name; nothing. Her matted fur gives off the potent odor of having lived in the wilds and garbage of wrecked suburbs and cities, constantly on the run from reivers and wild dogs.

"I'll call you Hepburn, because you have pluck and guts. Let's get out of here."

Back up through the thick underbrush and pebble-strewn dirt to the stony rail bed. The train awaits us, looming monolithically. I lift Hepburn up the steps and through an open door, into the passenger coach. She skitters down the aisle when I slam and latch the door. I get another glimpse of Loch Ness, which conveys a kind of sinister peacefulness. The monster has consumed more victims.

Hepburn curls up into a seat. I open the door to the driver's cab, where Terr sits, suppressing mild fury at our delay. He wants to get to London, vamonos.

"Have you finished the animal rescue duties?" he huffs.

"We're in. Ready to go!"

The train lurches forward before I have a chance to sit. Hepburn, thoroughly relaxed and trusting, sits on her hind quarters and gazes out the window at woods and wind-scoured mountain slopes. We make Inverness within the hour.

CHAPTER 28

Inverness offers no insurmountable obstacles. Terr is able to bypass the entire main train station and stay on open track, steering us south toward Perth and Edinburgh.

"We'll make Edinburgh in two hours," he says cheerily. "All systems go."

The dog slept soundly, as we streamed through a familiar landscape, Cairngorms National Park. A fog lifted, showing a bleak, undeveloped, and boundless land. A remote, beguiling terrain of bogs, heather, and mountains, even before the pandemic set in.

Inhospitable, gritty flatlands and sculpted mountains unfurled for miles on each side of the track.

I'd wanted to hike there with Will someday, but the infection killed him and our dreams.

I stared at the landscape through the window, letting my mind escape the calamities of recent months. All that was stolen from Will and I. He was definitely the camping and hiking type. I never got the chance to get to know that side of him, the one that wanted to lose himself in nature, with one companion by his side, not crowds. Just me.

The at times vacant and treeless landscape was as haunted as it was sublime. I saw Will's face reflected against the window and the clouds that smudged the sky, above the bluish green slopes, stretching to the horizon at least 50 miles.

I snap myself out of this self-pitying remorse. I can't forget, I have Terr My Hair and Hepburn; we're doing our level best at surviving, and more, especially Terr, who carries us along in a passenger coach. We still have days ahead to look forward to.

I put a little of the leftover salmon-oats mush into a bowl; set it on the seat beside her nose. I watch the half-starved dog's prominent ribcage move with her breathing. This must be the best she's eaten in months.

But how did she make it onto that boat? We'll never know; maybe it was the ferry to nowhere, and the people came down with H7N11 later.

We pass through Aviemore, a place that had a Scottish Highlands ski area, one of the few commercial ones in the U.K. I imagine its bare slopes, melting snow, and rubble. The abandoned T-bars and cables creaking in the wind. The empty restaurants and lodges reclaimed by mountains and nature.

All humanity and its trappings, I muse, are destined to be reclaimed by flora and fauna. We just don't think it will ever happen in our lifetimes, especially when we're living it up with other blind humans unconscious to the collapse and decay that lurks around the corner.

Revisiting strong emotions makes me sleepy. I nod off in the seat, keeling over onto my backpack. When I come to, I see the flat roofs and dirty facades and vehicle carcasses of a small city, Perth. The spire in the center of town is still there though, the wide lazy river and the picturesque castles near its shore.

I pity its lost classical history. I sense the superiority of someone just passing through an abandoned, dead place. Even a bombed city at the end of a war suggests renewal and rebuild. But I already have a train ticket out of this one.

Terr has slowed the train, weaving around steep curves and overpasses. I stare at the rooftops and the streets, into windows, searching for the uninfected, a human with a normal gait, a face expressing recognition, hope, awareness. I see nothing, not even a corpse.

I've become an expert on depopulated cities; no longer shocked by their still-life quality, their emphatic emptiness. The unsettling permanence of their vacancy.

Hectic urban life, in all its glory, glowing boulevards at night, crowded with bright young things fueled by wine and high on life. A jammed cafe with jazz and laughter in the air. It's a distant memory. I find my forehead leaning against the faintly soiled window, as I recall these things, like music I know by heart. Perth floats by and vanishes.

The train speeds up; I need an update from Terr. How soon to Edinburgh and London? Will we stop in Edinburgh at all?

I go make him some tea, with a hot plate plugged into an electrical outlet that runs off the diesel electric system. Ingenious.

Edinburgh would be crammed with food and supplies. It would be worth a stop. We could idle the train and score a lot more food, water, weed, and the like, if the place isn't infested with reivers. This is always a big if.

The dog gets up from the seat lethargically, stretches, then leaps into the aisle. Probably has to take a piss, or a shit. Her food is gone. I make a cup of English Breakfast and carry it to the driver's cab.

"Edinburgh soon…a few minutes," he says. Then "Thanks" when I hand him the tea. He takes it, places it on the dashboard above an elaborate control console. The cab is still impressive, with its lit up display screens and gauges, a reminder of former technological culture.

Wisps of steam rise from the cup. I hear a scratching on the door behind me. Hepburn is insistent and getting clingy with me.

"You know, the dog's got to…"

"Right," he nearly snaps. "We have to stop the whole train, just to walk the dog." I watch the track disappear beneath us, through his narrow windshield. We're passing through empty suburbs and green hills, with a glimpse of the North Sea, east of us.

We hit a rise, then down, and I view the smoking, arresting rooftops of the cityscape for the first time: Edinburgh.

CHAPTER 29

We roll into Edinburgh Waverley, the capital's main train station. I can't contain myself. All three of us are in the driver's cab, anticipating the big city arrival. We go from sunlit tracks to a sepulchral terminal, black hulks of idle carriages resting on adjacent platforms.

Terr hasn't flipped on his lamps yet. He plans to pull in temporarily, then back up and switch to a spur that aims us south toward London. He knows Waverley like the back of his hand.

At full stop, he floods the station with light.

Nothing moves. Only greasy, vacant platforms, overturned trash cans, and random debris spread around, as if gulls had left it there. I had expected much worse. I breathe a sigh.

Terr is all business.

"First and only stop for today, before London. Just let the dog pee, then let's get our arses outta here."

I look back at him perplexed. "Not narked," he says. "Just worried." The diesel-electric engine hums reassuringly.

"I promise I won't go far. Hepburn is going crazy. And I know of a market in the neighborhood where I can get some supplies."

"London has supplies…"

"We don't know what London has, or what's waiting for us there. We could use more food and medicine. Can you just sit tight for a few, my fine friend?"

"Yeah, just like the doomed ferry and your bloody animal rescue league. Well, I can't stop yah, can I? Just don't get stuck or chased by your reivers. Then I'll have to leave the train and…"

"Thirty minutes, max. Hepburn will do her thing, then I'll come back with a juicy bag of supplies. You'll thank me afterwards." Eyebrows rise with a weary skepticism, then he begins playing with the nobs and switches of the console, which is significantly computerized. He appears to take solace in it.

"I've got to go," I say.

Still looking away: "Be careful."

I've fashioned a leash from a short length of rope, which I tie around her remaining collar. We open the door and step down onto the platform. Hepburn immediately lifts her leg on a post nearby, then shakes herself out, tugs on the leash with renewed vigor. We head to the end of the platform and the entrance to the Waverley's waiting and ticketing area, which I know has an exit to Princes street.

We walk briskly along the greasy platform, my buff over my nose to block a pissy, subway-tunnel like odor. Yet, I'm surprised we've seen no bodies, or reivers. So far, from the windows of the train, the Scottish capital is vacant.

Terr appears on the top step, like a worried dad. "Twenty-eight minutes, and counting…"

"Right back!" I call out over my shoulder. Then we're off the platform, gingerly through the smashed glass of a disabled automatic door, and into the cluttered, echoing terminal.

I give it the once-over; an old renovated train station. There are pools of discolored water on the floor from burst pipes. A coffee and baked goods snack bar offers only charred remains.

I look up; the sun shines palely through an arched, ornate ceiling, which reminds me of a cathedral. A monument to the religion of travel and commerce, before the entire edifice had come crashing down, in only a matter of weeks.

The baroque ceiling is oddly untouched by end-of-world catastrophe.

I admire it for a moment, head tilted back, the sun touching my face. Hepburn tugs me toward the entrance for Princes Street. We cross the tiles and exit to the still life of Waverley's spacious paved courtyard. Only the sound of wind and the light flutter of blown newspapers, like leaves in a breeze.

The sun's rays pour over the tall rooftops across the street, lined with old soot-stained chimneys that look like black teeth.

In the air, I smell the sea. This makes the lost city seem alive again. I head downhill on Leith Street, towards where I used to know of a market and commercial block. I'm looking for food and medicine–that was my excuse for Terr–but this route also takes me past the hotel where I met Will. It feels both wistful and weird to experience it again.

We chatted then while waiting for the elevator, me in my cute dress and conference attire, feeling buoyant and professional. Such a casual way to meet. No classifieds, Facebook, or online dating for us.

It seems like half a century ago.

113

With Hepburn yanking on the leash, we half-run downhill. A tipped-over crane lays next to a hole in the ground behind chainlink fences. The carcasses of a bus, a black cab. Then we see the hotel, the empty cafe, still with soggy, limp umbrellas over black metal tables. Diners long gone. Calton Hill rises green and floral behind it, topped by the Scottish National Monument.

I pause on the sidewalk, make Hepburn sit. I knew this was going to happen. I can feel it well up in my chest, I still have Edinburgh and Will in my blood. But I don't anticipate getting clobbered like this.

Tears stream down my face; my chest heaves. I hear my whimpers, as though observing myself coldly from a distance. Hepburn sits idly and watches, head down. She wanders over and nuzzles my calf. Right there is the cafe where we sat in the sun and sipped wine, debating and solving the world's problems (little did we know…), letting time vanish unnoticed, as if only me and Will existed.

It was magic. Recalling that time makes it painful. It guts me.

He's gone sister, a practical voice intones. *Get over it.*

I snap out of it and we keep going. We're out on Princes Street, where I reach the smashed plate-glass windows of a ruined food market and pharmacy.

"You're going to have to stay outside, a few minutes." I tie Hepburn's leash to a parking meter, make her sit down. She promptly starts taking a poop, a good time for me to exit stage left, into the market, searching for food. The usual clutter and utter disarray. I don't expect to find much food that hasn't spoiled, but I've been surprised before.

Nothing like Gruyere and smoked salmon, but I do find boxes of powdered milk and potatoes (damn, I'm sick of these

114

freeze-dried potatoes), fistfuls of packaged beef jerky, and even a jar of Peter Pan peanut butter. I fish the boxes and packages off the floor that haven't gotten soggy and trod upon, then bag them.

At the end of the aisle, I find one of those multi-packs of colorful cereal from America: cellophane-wrapped Cheerios, Cocoa Puffs, Lucky Charms, Wheaties…at least they're calories. Into the bag they go.

That's when I hear the music, carried along the boulevard outside.

CHAPTER 30

I step outside with my supplies, turn toward the music. It's faintly audible from several blocks away. Jimmy Buffet's *Margueritaville.* So someone is here, I think, with enough intact consciousness to listen to music.

But I still have a pharmacy to search. This is the mother lode for me. It's adjacent to the market. I sidestep through a stuck revolving door and I'm passed the trashed cash register, which some determined soul has bludgeoned with a hard blunt object.

What possible value does money have anymore, in these desperate times?

Everything in a pharmacy has value, and I quickly load up on bandaids, gauze, medical tape, a tube of Bacitracin; several bottles of aspirin and ibuprofen, long expired in an official sense, but I know their potency lingers long after.

I snoop some more. I'm searching for CBD oil or tablets.

It's what I need the most. I remember that Hepburn waits outside. I hear her bark once, twice. I grab a plastic bottle of propylene glycol, still trolling the cluttered aisles. Toothpaste, soap, shampoo (that seems vain), a large-sized bottle of multivitamins. It all goes into the bag, which is beginning to get heavy.

My movements are loud and impulsive. I don't hear the music anymore.

There's no CBD to be found. Even without proof, I strongly believe CBD has kept me well. I look everywhere, until I am out of time. Terr is going to be so pissed. Then I hear Hepburn barking insistently, and the music again.

What happens next becomes one of my long journal entries.

Dated: April 16, 2028

This was one of my stranger, but more informative and dicey encounters, the way it evolved.

The music in Edinburgh originated from farther down Princes Street. I wondered if someone was still living there in survival mode. The sound seemed to come from the open window of an apartment. I untied Hepburn, threw the bag of goods over my back, and we marched toward the tunes.

Soon we reached an intersecting street, more like an alley. It used to be a pedestrian walkway and filled with lively pubs, restaurants, and cafes. The music was louder, having transitioned to London Is Calling by The Clash.

We turned into the alley. A block down was an outdoor cafe with a round table. Five people sat around it in a circle. I brandished my axe suspiciously, and we walked toward it.

I figured they're reivers in a dormant state. What else could they be? I was acutely aware of running out of time with

117

Terr, but I couldn't help myself. Me and Hepburn crept up to the table, and it's like they were all asleep.

Five old men, some with beards down to their belly buttons. An old cassette tape player, a real relic form the 20th century, sat on the table. It kept playing The Clash, until the run-down battery slowed the music and distorted the voices and instruments, giving the scene an even more surreal quality.

A finished bottle of Scotch sat in the middle of the table with five glasses and an empty prescription bottle. The potent, aromatic scent of weed was everywhere. Once closer, I noted the gray pallors and the unmistakable mien of death. The five men seemed peaceful; some even wore tired, rigid grins. They did it their way; it had to have been within the last few hours, I thought.

I'm out of time. Now I'm in big trouble with poor Terr, I thought. One of the bearded men's gnarled hand rested on a mailing envelope, which was addressed to someone. I removed and read it; To Whomever Finds These Jolly Old Sods Please Read.

The document was a computer printout. This guy had been a researcher. He'd been trying to study the disease. Then he caught it himself. A hero, I thought, dying trying to save the human race.

He said it was a prion-related disease that may have been related to Deer Wasting Syndrome, which had been rampant in deer, elk, and other cervids. He'd found no cure. The symptoms were obvious; mental decline, aggression in groups, then collapse, within about a week. It seemed to accelerate in women more. He knew of no unaffected females; this led him to believe that it was possibly a species-ending or -threatening virus.

A barebones team of scientists and other officials had

118

gathered ad hoc in London, literally to try to save the human race. They had been in communication with other groups, such as ones protecting the Seed Bank in Northern Norway. He left the address in London...

With the document, Me and Hepburn tried to hurry back to the train.

CHAPTER 31

The document goes into my bag, carefully. I then rifle all their pockets and come up with two half-empty ounce bags of weed. Scored them for Terr...and me. Maybe he won't be so mad.

Then I look up. I'm startled to see a feral-looking bloke standing and staring at me from the far end of the alley. He clutches a stick or a rod.

He's joined by one, two, three, four...all clutching staves or rods. They have shaved heads, look rather punky. Can't tell whether they're reivers. They start walking quickly toward us.

"Let's go!"

Me and Hepburn go into a half-run, barely. I can't manage more due to the weight of the pack. I carry the little axe in one hand.

"Shit shit!" I yell, knowing they're gaining on us. Down Princes Street we go. They're a half block behind us. I steal one look. They're going to catch us. Nowhere to run! I get the sudden guilty, defeatist thought: *Terr was right.* We never should have left the train.

We're marching up Leith Street now, past the empty construction site with the dead crane. They get closer, break into full runs, arms pumping and clutching staves. I grip the axe tightly in my right hand. At the top of the hill is the Waverley courtyard, but our sanctuary train is way too far for us to cover in time. It's through the terminal and onto the platforms.

This is going to end with a fight. I'm just about to let go of the leash to let Hepburn run; maybe she'll instinctively go for the train, maybe not.

I look behind me, five of them, with the telltale driven, lurching, stop-at-nothing gait; the contorted faces and menacing eyes. Clearly they're reivers. Off goes the backpack and I've got the axe in one hand, my feet in the ready position, my heart racing, sweat pouring down my face.

"Get outta here Hepburn!" Good that'll do…she stays by my side.

The one in front makes a wretched cry and raises what looks like a rebar over his head…then I notice in my peripheral vision a form step out into the courtyard.

"Welcome to Waverley."

A huge pop and roar like a dozen cherry bombs. Then a swarm of metal pellets hits the attacking reiver and creams him backward off his feet, spraying blood. Terr empties the other barrel of the shotgun, the pellets striking two of the others. Down they go.

The hot, tart scent of cordite floods my nostrils. My ears ring. I reach down and seize the backpack off the ground.

Three of the reivers lie in the courtyard, bleeding and

twitching. Two others stop in their tracks, then begin the aimless wandering. It's obvious what's happening.

The first thing I can think of saying is, "Where did you get that shotgun!"

"It's always been around. I just didn't bother to tell you."

"Thank you. I mean, for saving me arse again. I think I was over-matched."

"You *think*?" he says, with more than a little scorn. Then gently: "Where would I be if they got to you? Alone again. Do you think I'd let that happen?"

"No," I say sheepishly.

He turns and heads purposefully for the terminal and the train. Dazed and confused, the two other reivers wander off into the middle of Princes Street. Hepburn, who'd dashed halfway across the courtyard during the shotgun blasts, returns with her tail between her legs and follows us, dragging her leash.

Hepburn is apparently not the fierce protective type of mutt, but her survival instincts are above average.

"I got some good stuff!" I call out, sort of trying to make up for pulling us into more trouble. Terr looks back at me, unimpressed. Rifle hanging at his side. No comment.

"Including weed…" That stops him in his tracks.

"Really? Pot?"

"Truly." We wander through the mess of the waiting area, voices echoing hollowly.

"Where did you get it?" he says, still walking back to his beloved train.

"Out of the suit coats of a couple of old men. They'd had a last dinner, all of 'em passed away. I smelled the pot like they'd smoked a joint within the hour, so I went through their pockets."

"How enterprising. What else did you find?"

"I found their last letter. At least one of them was a scientist. It describes some hold-out group in London, trying to save us humans. He'd done some research on H7N11. Said it was a prion-based disease that had no cure."

"Shit, I could 'o told 'em that. What's a prion?"

"It's a poison protein…attacks the brain. I have the address in London."

He shrugs. We reach the greasy platforms. Terr mounts the carriage steps and folds the door aside. Hepburn stops and pees on the platform first. Smart, I think. I believe I'm finished walking her around Edinburgh for now.

We're in the train, safely behind closed doors. The first thing Terr says, after he stores the weapon in a compartment above his head: "Now get the weed out, will you?"

We open the window out of habit, and I take out the zip-locked bags containing the dry, powdered hooch. I open the bag. The aroma is rich and fecund, like fresh ground coffee.

"I got a pipe," Terr chirps, a bit too eagerly. He's really missed smoking weed. I think he was a real dopehead, through no fault of his own. He had injuries. And it probably saved him from H7N11.

Endocannabinoid receptors in the brain are bound by CBD, THC, and other cannabinoids, preventing H7N11 from binding receptors, using brain matter as a host, and slowly destroying brain cells…I almost can hear my own presentation…

Rich, green, thick smoke fills the cabin. The bowl of Terr's pipe glows with pot. He puffs away. The chaw of weed glints on and off, his eyes are closed. He exhales…ahhh, that smell.

He seems rather mesmerized. Then he removes the pipe from his mouth, hands it to me.

"It's fine–real good. I'm chuffed," he says, voice constricted in a way that reminds me of adolescence. Puffing weed with friends in the woods.

I have a taste, it makes me cough right away. There's a little hurt in the back of my throat. My voice is constricted, too.

"Don't you think we should have gotten the train going first? What about the reivers out there?"

He's sure of himself. "I'm gettin' high and have me a nap, then we're on to London."

I've got no argument. I feel the buzz come on.

My second inhalation is gentler. I'm easy–it has an immediate effect…everything slows down, I smile ear to ear, and so does Terr.

We start laughing.

CHAPTER 32

"Remember the look on the bloke's face, raising his stave, like he's some kind of goofy, half-assed knight?" Terr laughs and smoke comes out of his nose. We dissolve into giggles.

The outside world seems to melt away. We are laughing about a forbidden topic, an infected person who's basically dead.

The magic and the presumptuousness of the drug is that you can laugh uproariously about the horror. All life becomes theater of the absurd. For the moment at least, it's an effective refuge from the true awfulness of our plight.

I'm buzzed, to say the least. Terr, who had been grumpy during the trip so far, begins to assume a rogue charm. I like his rough good looks, a bit like the old actor Russell Crowe. Terr's also my hero of the month, if not the years. I move on to the seat next to his and put my hand around his shoulder. We pass the pipe back and forth– I am clearly out of my gourd. I don't even want to think about the Scotch. Add that and I'll be on the deck, taking a ten count.

"You don't think we should make sure that the doors are…locked?" We look around the carriage for a moment, then burst out laughing in red-faced guffaws. A thin curtain of dissipating pot smoke hovers close to the ceiling.

Hepburn has slunk down to the end of the carriage. I don't think she likes the powerful odor. First cordite and ear-splitting roars, then this…

Reading the part of the scientist's letter about the women disturbed me to no end, I think, bemused and getting sleepy. Even stoned I couldn't hurl that notion from my mind. *70 percent of immediate victims female…no women found alive in a year–species ending…the dominance of initial female victims is certainly another hot topic for scientists probing H7N11.*

When I'd raced through that looted pharmacy, I'd even grabbed a box of Lifestyles condoms, purely out of instinct. And in memory of Will. That was our brand. Sometimes he'd get Trojans. It didn't really matter to me.

What mattered back then was not getting pregnant by mistake. Was that a decision that actually affected our species?

Now I go back to an earlier entry in my journal, about two and a half years Before Carnage:

Dated: March 21, 2024

Will and I don't talk about kids in our future, but he's my fiancee and it's definitely an elephant in the room. We're going to try for kids someday. I'm convinced of that. We use condoms mostly now, though. Where my career is now with W.H.O., and my research, I cannot get pregnant. That would be the kiss of death for what I'm doing. I'm just not the type who can work hard at a busy office, and deal with pregnancy. I'm also someone who relies on being in control, and to me, getting pregnant willy-nilly is the essence of out of control!

So I pay attention to my physical rhythms and we seldom, but sometimes, have unprotected sex. Lifestyles and Trojans; but we both prefer unprotected free.

This is an ongoing discussion because Will has to have sex most nights, before he goes to sleep. I don't always feel like it, but the only time he abstains is when he's tired.

So two months ago, I'm late on my period. This is unusual, because normally I'm like clockwork. I was a bit on edge. A few weeks go by, and still no period. For once, I actually wanted to experience some bleeding.

Now I'm really nervous, all kinds of notions swirling through my head. I have to get tested. I confide in Will. He's quietly pleased, and cannot not disguise it. This makes me, in turn, quietly furious that, as a typical guy, he doesn't appreciate what a momentous event pregnancy is, what it means for a woman with a complex life. Or any woman for that matter. He just thinks of himself as some sort of chest-beating, fertile he-man.

I. Got. Her. Pregnant. Whippy ding.

Do I really want to know if I'm pregnant? I think, supremely vexed. What if I am? Then what? As it's in my nature, I start the "what-if" decision-making. The scientific method. Maybe I'm just too obsessive compulsive but...

The pregnancy would be in its earliest stages. Therefore, I would seek to induce an abortion. There are far fewer consequences in the first trimester; in fact, a small number of pregnancies naturally terminate then. It's terrible, in a way, to think about it, but making children with Will has to be planned in a rational way, and ending the pregnancy was what I plan to

127

do.

I didn't tell Will. I was afraid he'd be crestfallen about my decision, then push back on it.

With a lump in my throat, I do the quick and easy pee-on-the-wand test: negative. I make sure at a Planned Parenthood clinic. No pregnancy. It's stress, primarily, that's delayed the period.

But that decision to terminate the pregnancy with Will has always haunted me. I would have gone ahead with ending it. A certain uncompromising determination to do it–I was getting ready to resist Will's predicted efforts to the contrary–bothers me. It's as if my thinking process revealed an uncomfortable truth about myself.

Now that precise decision-making has implications for the species. There must be another woman walking around uninfected *somewhere.* But there's no evidence in either North America or Europe that there are any other normal healthy females. The entire world has been decimated by H7N11. I might be, could be, hypothetically, the last.

CHAPTER 33: FOUR MONTHS LATER; AUGUST 2028

We're settled in London. King's Cross station is a cozy place for the train, and even though we're surrounded by thousands of vacant domiciles, we see no need to move. Besides, many of the more spacious places were high-rises where the elevators don't work.

It's tempting to move to an empty stretch of flats on a park, which might be a future consideration, but there are still reivers out and about (not nearly at the density of the Isle Of Skye though), and scarily, roving packs of dogs and coyotes at night.

At first glance, London is remarkably intact. Sure, it has an unsettling quietude during the day, which causes me to hear the voices inside my head of hundreds of thousands of people who aren't there. The night is inky and impenetrable. Black walls on all sides, blocking out the starlight, and windows that proffer no light, in a way that Skye never was.

But the pandemic caused nothing like the London Blitz. The Tower Bridge, and most other landmarks, still stand tall. The London Eye, a popular ferris wheel, sits by the Thames in the sunshine. It creaks in a high wind like a giant, rusty weather vane.

The river flows green, deep, and eternal beneath Waterloo Bridge, Black Friars, and Southwark.

It's simple to find provisions. By this point, I'm an expert at looting markets, which of course abound in the vast city. I ride a bike around town, from King's Cross north of the Thames, through Covent Garden, then along the Thames to London Bridge. Hitting markets and cluttered stores along the way.

There are of course, no Black Cabs or double-decker buses or horse-drawn carriages to imperil me on the road. It's like riding alone in the countryside, but surrounded by really tall buildings. There are abandoned bikes all over the place, and we harvest those, including the wheels, chains, chainrings, and other parts.

I carry a handgun now. I got it from Terr, who took it off a dead policeman. I haven't had to use it yet. Ammo is a problem, and I only have a nine-bullet clip. But we remember what happened at Waverley Station in Edinburgh, and if it comes down to wild coyotes, reivers, or me, I'll use it.

Terr showed me how to take the safety off and aim it, gripping it in two hands, then pull the trigger.

There is still no evidence of intact communications systems. No internet servers, no radio signals, and certainly all cable broadcasts are dead. The airwaves have gone silent, as have the heavens.

No jets ply the skies. The blue canopy over London radiates the purity and calm of a painted canvas. Clouds like broad white brushstrokes applied to an azure vault. I often gaze up at the silent sky from one of the many overgrown gardens thriving in London's lost side streets.

Then the rains and dank mist and grayness that I also remember of London will come. I'll take refuge with my bike beneath the tattered remnants of a pub's umbrella, or a restaurant's outdoor canopy.

I'll watch the moisture flow down the gutter that, unmaintained, has filled with mud and pebbles. The vehicle, bus, and truck wrecks are like moss-covered boulders in the wide riverbeds of Southwark Street, Waterloo Road, Upper Thames Street, and the rest.

Wildlife has migrated into the weed-covered, placid shell of a city. Terr hunted for rabbit and opossums near the Princess Diana Memorial Fountain. Deer were around, but too risky to eat.

We eat very well, considering, given the occasional treats like game, my scavenging for canned, boxed, and bottled edibles, and even tomatoes, squash, peas and the like, which we grow in a garden near King's Cross.

We're eating way beyond emergency rations–including copious multivitamins that I harvest from smashed pharmacies.

Survival is very hard work. We don't stay up late, normally. We eat as the sun goes down, then sleep. We walk Hepburn, prepare a decent dinner, sip a little wine or Scotch, and usually toke up. The black night curtains outside, but we are cozy behind locked doors.

London, which in recent years had legalized pot, is full of dispensaries where we can still find high-quality weed. It will run out eventually, however.

Understanding its protective qualities, I have no problem drifting into pot-headedness. I don't want any neurological decay, however, which can come from too much marijuana, so I take many breaks.

It's surreal, occupying London as if we're the only ones living there. We encounter no healthy people. The reivers are distributed thinly throughout the cityscape and commonly, they have declined to the aimless-wandering-to-collapse stage. But that doesn't mean there aren't still some herded, dangerous ones.

As I mentioned, the city has developed a hazardous wild-dog problem. Terr thinks they're coywolves, a hybrid of wolves and coyotes. This means Hepburn, now a cherished and dependable companion, can never run free. But she has plenty of walks and enjoys a can of dog-food per day, along with the rabbit, including organ parts, when such is available.

I'm hungry as a horse all the time, especially for high-cal foods, fat, and quality meat. The latter is often slim pickings.

The time has come for us to set out and find this supposed colony of species-rescue and survival researchers. The address is a building in Southwark not far from the Thames and the Tower Bridge.

We walk Hepburn, lock her in the train, then mount our bikes, heading for the Thames and Southwark. I've been down in these neighborhoods before, but now we're making a concerted effort to find healthy people. My skin tingles with excitement, a desire to hear new voices and break out of our rigid state of barebones survival.

I sense something momentous is going to happen. Not fraught with peril, but with good tidings. Still, I bring my handgun. You can never be too sure in these parts.

I'm strapped, as Terr puts it.

CHAPTER 34

It's a nice morning, but you can tell rain is coming in the afternoon. Clouds like soggy cotton balls gather over Westminster. Rain is something we're used to; it's just water (which we often collect in buckets and bowls), and it reminds us of the past.

We ride south to Upper Thames Street, which traverses the river past old piers and boat clubs and stone federal buildings fallen into disrepair. We stop and dismount at the Tower Bridge for a water break.

We're going to cross the river here. The bridge is reasonably clear of debris, and the bikes give us a mobility we wouldn't have in a vehicle.

Beneath us is the Tower Of London. I sip water from a plastic bottle and gaze down into the now unkempt grounds behind the walls. Weeds and dried-out dirty patches have replaced the immaculate lawns; the once preserved catapult lies in pieces. Still, it's a very large, uninhabited residence with a secure wall around it.

Maybe we can live there?

Terr stands next to his bike drinking from his own bottle, staring across the river. Dark office buildings and hotels; an old gray battleship that was set aside for tourists. The vessel lies still moored and unchanged. The deep Thames is the dull muddy green of floodwaters.

"What do you think about moving into the Tower?"

"You're not serious." He looks around the city absently, as if jogging his memory for landmarks and seminal events from the past.

"We'd be safe behind the walls, and so much space inside..."

"Are you getting homemaker urges? Too many ghosts for me...Lady Jane Grey...William Wallace. You being Scottish, you want to live in the place where they tortured William, then stuck his head on a pike and put it on Tower Bridge?"

"Literally, ancient history."

"We *have* a good place to live."

"We do, but four miles from Central London–there's limitless supplies to harvest down here."

"There's more of *everything* here. Coywolves...the daft bastards...I like our relatively quiet neighborhood."

Rather than locks horns with Terr, I decide to let the topic go for now.

Over the cluster of roofs across the Thames, a tall building stabs the sky. It looks only partially finished on top, like a chunk of it broke off and tumbled to the ground. A spiky pinnacle decorates its peak. It's a striking contrast to the ancient walls of the tower in the foreground.

"What's that tall building? Looks like a giant knife."

"That's the Shard. We ought to get going."

I guzzle my water bottle, insert it back in its holder, mount the bike. We pedal amiably through the light breeze across the Tower Bridge, like two Londoners, circa 2023, coattails and scarves flapping, calmly making their way to office jobs.

How utterly different this actually is.

We take a right on Tooley Street across the bridge. It's narrow and cluttered, with diagonally stalled vehicles and the usual mass of mud, leaves, and trash. Passing abandoned restaurants in the Tooley neighborhood, all the wonderful places–Magdelenas, Brigade, Santo Remedio, Jamie's Italian– my stomach growls with memories of lavish meals out. Even though the windows are shattered and their awnings are ripped up, and the charm is all but gone.

On the way back, I vow to loot those kitchens. Chief Pillager and Looter, that's me. I'm actually proud of my ability to sift edible calories and potable water from the dross of the spoiled crap I find in most of those places.

It's a skill, scavenging and survival; it truly is. They used to derisively refer to part of what I do as "dumpster diving" or "amateur prepping." But it's no joke. That's one of the things I've learned.

Terr is ungainly and awkward on a bike, but game. I tire a little easier than before; par for the course. We cut across on Strand Street to St. Thomas, dismount, walk our bikes to the address. 112 St. Thomas Street, as specified in that old man's letter from Edinburgh.

This is where the scientists are supposed to be holed up, trying to save the world.

I find 112. It's a brick home, and a wreck. Door splintered and hanging on one hinge, windows smashed, scorch marks marring the brick from a second-floor window.

135

I walk up to the front door; a God awful smell wafts out. Something gross is spilled in the doorway.

"No one's home in this dump," I call out. We double-check the address, it's correct. I gaze up and down the street, for a lost moment. The last thing I want to do is give up on these people, if they exist.

"That's The Shard, the St. Thomas Street exit," Terr says absently. "87 floors. Glass and steel tower. Might be worth checking out, for the stuff…do your looting, you know…"

"For what? Computers that don't work and stacks of office paper? Isn't it just fancy offices?"

"Hotel and restaurants, too. Knew someone who stayed there once. Swanky. Get a 50th floor room with a 180-degree view of London."

I gaze straight up at the glass tower, windows still reflecting the sky, as if they're painted a radiant blue. About 20 floors up hangs a metal platform with railings. A system of ropes and cables are suspended from it.

"Window washers?" I say, pointing up to it. Terr, weary, sits down on a wall where his bike leans.

That's when we see someone step out from an opening in one of the windows. A pane of hard glass swings outwards, and a person emerges. A female. She boards the platform carefully. It begins to slowly descend to the street level on its roped pulley system.

Absolutely not a reiver, I think. Her motions are too purposeful and coordinated, in sync with this relatively sophisticated platform. And even more amazing, she's a gal!

CHAPTER 35

Terr and I exchange intense and keen glances, then walk our bicycles quickly to the street level beneath the Shard.

When I get closer, I see the lady has tied-back white hair, a purple T-shirt, with a sweater looped around her waste. Thrilled at the notion of interacting with another young female, I find her age vaguely disappointing.

Beggars can't be choosers. We haven't run into healthy people in more than a year.

When the platform reaches street level, it pauses, she unlatches a metal gate, then stiffly exits onto the sidewalk. Terr and me walk quickly down the center of St. Thomas Street pushing our bikes.

I yell out: "Hey lady! M'am! M'lady!" I wave my arms, but for a moment she makes eye contact and appears horrified. Who's to blame her? We stop. I cry out loud enough to be heard, but not frantically.

"We're healthy survivors. We're looking for others like us. Can we come closer?"

She looks at me as though she's seen a ghost, then she makes a half-wave, come-hither gesture. We cover the remaining half block, set our bikes down. I hold out my hand.

"Emma Wallace. This here's Terry Winslow."

"Greta Forger," she replies evenly, with more suspiciousness than warmth. We shake hands. Hers is knobby and arthritic.

"Where did you come from?" she asks.

"King's Cross," Terr says. "We live on a train. We took it down from the Isle Of Skye."

"You rode on a train?" Greta asks incredulously.

"It's a long story…he's a master trainman. The main thing is, we found you. I'm so happy to make your acquaintance."

Understandably, she remains suspicious, with a flat and somber mood. I take her to be in her early to mid-Seventies. White wispy hair, pronounced wrinkles at the corners of her mouth and eyes. She regards me with a curious wonder and slightly rheumy eyes.

The Shard looms above us monolithically, an errant breeze whipping around its sharp corners and rattling the cables hanging off the platform nearby.

"Are you one of the scientists?" I ask.

"I'm an assistant. How did you know about us?"

"From an older gentleman in Edinburgh. He'd passed away, but he left a letter."

She continued to look at me with amazement.

"Have either of you been sick?"

"Had me a cold two months ago," Terr says, more in the way of making conversation. He seems bored with the turn of events. "Couldn't shake it with the stress and all. Could 'a been

138

hay fever…"

She gives him a faintly patronizing look.

"No, I mean, any symptoms from the pandemic: the headaches, confusion. Have you recently been exposed to infected people, close up? Because we can't risk killing the scientists we have. We're down to just two, and me."

I put it firmly. "No. If we could be infected, it would have happened months ago."

She looks at both of us warily, from one to the other. We've really got her spooked. She must be half batty, I think, with being frail and all, and holed up in that Shard.

"I have a garden half a block down. Come with me," she says, beginning her old-lady's shuffle.

"Garden…nice," I say. "We can help you with that. It would be a pleasure."

Then she begins to lighten up. "I'm sorry to stare, but you're the only young female I've encountered since the first month of the pandemic. They're all gone. Do you know what that means?"

"Of course I do. I can't escape the implications, can I? Don't you imagine that it's been kind of weighing on me for the last year, when I haven't been fighting the reivers…"

"The what?" Her voice is a cranky, dodgy squeak.

"Reivers. It's what I call the violent infected, when they group up and roam around."

"You mean the physically violent and herding behaviors exhibited by infected people."

"Except under no circumstances are them *people* any more," Terr adds, to which the lady raises her eyebrows in suspicion. She looks away, perhaps embarrassed that she could disapprove of our bluntness.

I'm thinking, maybe she spent too much time behind ivy-covered walls. She can't call a spade a spade anymore.

"Humans have no way to reproduce anymore," she says, changing the subject. As if that hadn't already occurred to us. She pauses, then looks me up and down. "Are you healthy, otherwise? You look fit and healthy. You must be a real survivor type."

"That's what I've become."

At this point, Terr spots something that genuinely seizes his attention. A newer looking motorcycle, compared with the vehicle wreckage that surrounds us.

"That's a Harley Davidson," he says, veering away to cross the street. "A recent vintage…in decent shape…at least, from what I can see from here." He heads for the bike like a kid going for his Christmas presents.

"For God's sake, don't go near that body!" Greta cries after him. A moldering corpse, clad head to toe in black faux leather, lies on a sidewalk not far from the bike.

"No worries," Terr answers, with undisguised irritation. "You gotta gather what still works in this world. And ignore the dead." He's all over the bike in minutes, like an art collector and a prized sculpture.

"I'm healthy and strong," I say proudly. "Don't get sick generally. Obviously, I'm not infected." Terr's now out of range of my voice.

"And I'm four months pregnant."

CHAPTER 36

"Roughly four months. I can't know for sure, but I'm 90 percent certain. No period. Morning sickness, all over now. Showing a bit on the tummy."

It all came out, speaking with a female. Almost against my will.

Greta gapes at me in amazement. She treats me like I'm some kind of alien from another planet.

"A woman knows," I add.

"She certainly does."

We reach the entrance to a park and community garden, more accurately, a riot of weeds and flowers with veggies hidden in them. Around the corner is the boulevard that intersects with London Bridge. I still haven't gotten used to the famed formerly busy intersections that appear now like deserted graveyards.

Terr is busy examining the Harley about half a block away.

"I'm going to harvest a few things," Greta says. "Can you hold the bag for me? I'll drop them in." There's something I can't quite put my finger on: a bossy, pushy way of asking for your help, even with little things.

She talks as she removes a few squashes and pumpkin-colored tomatoes. "How are you eating?"

"We have enough food, but I'm hungry all the time. It's cool."

"Do you know what this means?" she says excitedly, shutting the gate to the garden. We walk slowly back toward the Shard entrance. "This is the first time I've felt…a surge in optimism, in months."

Her tone suggests that I'd gotten pregnant mostly for her sake. For the furthering of her agenda. "It gives us a sense of the future, a way out of this nightmare. We've communicated with some people in Norway, responsible for the Seed Bank. They know of no other living female of child-bearing age. You're virtually…Mitochondrial Mary."

"Who the Hell is that?" I'm losing patience with her schtick. This is my baby, only mine.

"We all have mitochondrial DNA. Inside the mitochondria, the DNA comes only from your mother. In humans, all of that DNA derives ultimately from one female, generations ago in Africa. She's referred to, fondly, as Mitochondrial Mary."

Fascinating, but maybe not so. What's she getting at?

"All I am is a young lass who thinks she's pregnant. And I'm not even half way there. I see nothing more to it than that."

"Oh by God there *is* more to it than that. The human race has nowhere to go from here, without future generations."

Maybe the human race hasn't earned the right to go any farther, given what it's maybe inflicted on itself. I understand the hypocrisy implicit in my thoughts. I don't care about humans, but I will certainly care for a baby.

I look for Terr. There he is, sitting astride the motorcycle, smiling, still like a kid on Christmas. It's only about the fourth working vehicle we've found, and those were four-wheel cars almost out of fuel.

"Let's go back to the Shard," she says. "Colin will bring us up. He got the outside elevator to work. It keeps breaking, though. Then we take the stairs."

"Who's Colin?"

"He's one of the scientists."

"What kind of scientist?"

"A physicist."

"Do you have any doctors?"

"No. There's only one other scholar, and he's also a physicist, a specialist in particle theory. He's my husband Mal." Then she looks at me avidly. "We'll have a feast when we get up there, in honor of the new Mom."

"You seem pretty confident that I'm actually pregnant." *Almost wishful thinking. She's too excited, as if it's a wonderful event for her, not me.*

"As you said, a woman knows. I can, for lack of a better term, examine you…"

"I'm good," I say, killing the prior offer as quickly as I can.

A loud cough disturbs the placid silence of the emptied city. A dark acrid smoke cloud from a cold engine temporarily drifts over the sidewalk. Terr, grinning ear to ear, rolls away from the curb and heads down the block in the other direction.

"Just taking her for a spin," he yells out, passing us on St. Thomas Street.

"Oh good," I say. "Another valuable resource. A source of transportation." I wonder what angry hornets the noisiness might disturb, however, as London has been unusually quiet

143

today. I don't want to wake up any reivers.

"I suppose so," Greta says noncommittally, as if Terr was a juvenile delinquent. She still seems to dislike him because of his comment dehumanizing the reivers, or maybe merely because he's a less educated male.

The reivers are nothing but a hideously diseased brain driving two arms and two legs, I reiterate to myself. To think of them as the people they once were is both inaccurate and naive. Their souls are gone. *Arrivederci.* There's no cure. We have to man-up to that fact.

Greta seems to want to change the subject from Terr, and have him ride away forever into the sunset.

"Do you know who the father is?"

I only hesitate a moment. *The nosey old crank.* "No."

"No? How couldn't you, under these circumstances?"

I straighten my shoulders defiantly. "It's none of your business."

She's taken aback, not used to someone pushing against her probes. Especially in these desolate parts.

"Very well. Sorry I asked. What matters most, I suppose, is that you're pregnant and healthy."

We reach the cage system, which rests at the bottom of the looming facade. I *am* hungry. Terr turns around at the end of St. Thomas and motors back to us, legs outstretched in the manner of Dennis Hopper in *Easy Rider*. Terr's been able to escape the misery of the pandemic's aftermath for a brief moment of long lost man play.

I still wonder if it's even worth it following this pushy lady to her perch in the Shard.

"What have you guys discovered?" I ask. "What do you know about what other survivors are doing? Do you have any communications?"

"The men have a radio set up. They've communicated with some people in Norway and Australia. There, and especially in New Zealand, still have pockets of people. We don't know much more, but we will! Again, no mention of young females."

Can we move on from that subject...? I think.

Terr has shut the engine off and put down the kickstand. He's brimming with excitement.

"Run's great! Purrs like a kitten."

"How much gas?" I ask.

"Plenty!"

CHAPTER 37

Me and Terr decide to head up the Shard. I can at least get a solid meal out of it, and share my CBD-theory of immunity. That way it could be disseminated to the remaining far-flung survivors, including in the Antipodes and Scandinavia.

Terr parks the Harley nearby, and we climb onboard the cage system. There's a jolt. It starts to rise. I allow myself the pleasure of the view, the muddy artery of the Thames, the spacious green parks of Westminster. The pleasing angles of the formidable but lightless skyline.

Parks flourish all over the place. The forest was beginning to take over in London, slowly reclaiming the city streets.

"Why did you ever move to this place?" I ask Greta, who clings precariously to the railing.

"We lived near the garden–but there were too many hazards down below," she says, trying to make herself heard above the metallic ratcheting noise of the cage. "Dogs and rats, mostly…Colin broke in here, climbed the stairs, and we found this intact residence on the 20th floor."

I nod with understanding. They appear to be above average at scavenging and homesteading, if not in my and Terr's league.

"How many people did you start out with?"

"Eight, a year ago…"

Ouch. So they've lost five of the originals.

"Did everybody get sick?"

"No, not all. Three left. They found a van. Thought they could do better north of here," she says dismissively. *So this brainy survival clan wasn't as tight as the old man's letter appeared to imply. Greta's pompous and prickly air probably drove them off.*

We're about 200 feet above the ground, and the system stops with a jolt that almost knocks us off our feet. I watch the Thames again, somewhat transfixed with the sluggish current, which I can still perceive from blocks away. The endless flow to the sea, oblivious to the lamentable affairs of men, is predictable and calming.

No vessels have set sail on it, but plenty are still moored along its shores. That's something to keep in mind, if London doesn't prove promising. We could take a barge to the sea, maybe head for France. I keep dreaming up alternatives, even though the here and now could be a lot worse.

Storm clouds gather over Stamford Bridge, then I feel a light refreshing spray in the air.

A window unlatches, swings out like a door. A bearded man in a dark T-shirt and tattered bluejeans stands on the other side. He unlatches a gate for us and beckons us in. His hair is streaked with gray but he looks quite a bit younger than Greta.

He has a welcome smile. We step into the Shard at last,

entering the remnants of a fancy hotel lobby with a 270-degree view of London.

On the far wall hangs an elaborate oriental tapestry. A half-circle, hardwood desk looks like where the checkin used to be. Now it's covered with yellowed *Daily Mails* and *London Times*. Tables and chairs from the former restaurant are still arrayed along the windowed walls with their long view of London, now shrouded with wet cottony clouds.

Greta whispers in Colin's ear. It's an awkward moment, before formal introductions, and I guess she's telling him I'm pregnant. That appears to be an almost holy topic in these parts. It unnerves me. Pisses me off actually. *Keep your noses out of my personal business!*

Another table nearby already has a nice spread of food on it. We shake hands, they beckon us to sit down there.

Without a moment's hesitation, I seize a couple of crackers and make a ham and cheese sandwich out of them. Shove 'em in my mouth. I'm ravenous, eating lustily. The food reminds me of the chunks of cheese I recovered from the Cullin Hills on Skye, which Terr and I finished weeks ago.

"Where the hell did you get this feast?" I ask.

Terr smiles, chewing slowly. "And I thought I'd be the one without table manners..."

"No, please, eat up," Greta says warmly. "You must be starved. Emma here needs her nutrients. Her calories."

What am I, a fatted calf, getting primed for the juiciest cut?

"What did you do before the pandemic?" Colin asks me.

In my muffled voice: "I was a virus researcher for the World Health Organization in New York."

"Really? Wow! So I assume you have some theories about H7N11?"

"I do."

"And they're working so far? Since neither one of you are sick, as far as we know."

"They *are* working," I say, my cheeks still full of half chewed crackers and cheese. Colin pours me a glass of water and pushes it in front of me.

"What about you guys?" I ask. "How come you and Greta have stayed well so far?"

Colin clasps his hands in front of him and makes a steeple. "Luck, in part. We basically quarantined ourselves from the infected masses, from the very beginning. We tried strategies until we hit upon one and it worked. We've been taking massive vitamin C supplements, in tablet and liquid form. Thousands of milligrams per day. Pretty easy to find if you search the pharmacies. When we both felt sickness coming on a few months ago, we took it intravenously."

"You have the apparatus here for that?"

"Yes. I can't prove that this works, but we're not sick. What's your own theory about the pathogen? Is it potentially curable?"

"No, not if it reaches a certain stage. It's a virus similar to the wasting diseases that used animals as hosts: Deer Wasting Disease, Mad Cow Disease. CBD and other cannabinoids help stop the virus from binding to brain cells. That, and hormesis early in life."

"What do you mean by hormesis?"

"Exposure to virulent pathogens early in life, and surviving them."

"Interesting," Colin says, tapping his finger on the table. "So you take a lot of CBD? That must be hard to come by..."

"Harder than weed. Greta said you've been in touch with some people in Australia, Norway. That's pretty ingenious, to get communications like that."

149

He waves the achievement away modestly. "We have a radio. Plus, someone's got a few web servers up on a generator, like the cage system outside. But most of the network is dead space."

I see an opportunity to spread my theory around, which I'm about 80 percent confident in. It makes me feel like I have a purpose beyond merely living through another day, me and the baby that is. Even though I dread the days ahead, as a pregnant lass without a hospital, as difficult and perilous.

CHAPTER 38

"Tell them in Australia and Norway, and wherever else, take CBD oil under the tongue, smoke your weed, chow marijuana brownies, whatever...it can prevent them from getting fatally infected. This advice can save people."

"Will do. You're the one with the credentials–in fact, I can't think of anyone walking around uninfected on earth who has better credentials, or is more important to humanity, than you."

Not exactly sure what he meant by that, but it seems to be another cryptic reference to my pregnancy. I begin robotically eating pieces of chopped up tomatoes and onions with the crackers, forcing us to change the subject.

The windows flow with rivulets of rain from the storm. The clouds are like a low-lying fog, shrouding everything beneath the 20th floor. It reminds me of looking outside a plane's window to the cushiony layer of clouds.

"Where do you live in here?"

"We have dozens of rooms to choose from on this floor. You're free to occupy them. We'd love to have you join us. We have to stick together, the uninfected. For our own survival, not to mention, for the sake of the human race."

Terr stands up abruptly, wipes cracker crumbs from the corners of his mouth with his hand. "I'm grateful for the food, it really hit the spot. But we have a dog. He's waiting for us up at Somers Town."

They don't know we're living at King's Cross. They don't *have* to know.

"We'll be off now. But if you don't mind, I'll have a quick look around. It's not often you get a high view of London these days. For me, this is a rare treat…for once to the manor born, if you get my drift."

He walks away from the table towards a door leading to the residential suites, next to a defunct elevator. Then he disappears inside a hallway. The door closes.

Thick Plexiglass panes surround us, proffering a view of gray empty buildings like decrepit monuments over London Bridge. Greta and Colin are seated across from me. They make me uncomfortable. I stand up and cross over to the windows, tracing a path with my eyes across the Thames and back to the train.

I still don't quite believe I'm on the 20th floor of a hotel, when I see a man in shirtsleeves, staggering and aimless, cross the Bridge. Towards our side of the Thames, but clearly he has no destination in mind. He has a drunken gait and looks to face-plant on the concrete at any moment. He's one of the first reivers I've seen in London, other than the recently deceased.

"It's a person!" I cry out.

Greta moves to the window and says, "don't watch!" There

are people behind the man, a herd, rushing across the Bridge from the other side. Maybe a dozen of them bolt madly across the Bridge, like a *banzai* attack of mindless automatons. But it's only H7N11 at work. I can't take my eyes off them. I cover my mouth with my hand; they reach the staggering man, hurl him to the pavement, and beat him savagely, tearing at his clothes and clubbing him with both fists.

"Emma, don't," I hear Greta behind me. "That's why we moved up here." By now I'm crying, tears streaming down my cheeks, convulsive sobs making my chest heave and my arms tremble. It feels like I'm crying for the sick, the dead, and the future unknown.

These barking mad pregnancy emotions I'm going to have to deal with. They're only going to get more intense.

A few days later, I share a spot of sunshine with Hepburn, on a bench in King's Cross' empty, windswept courtyard, writing in my beloved journal. As usual, I have a lot to say, for anyone who stumbles across this dramatic account in the future. If we have one.

CHAPTER 39

Dated: August 30, 2028

After Colin brought up my pregnancy, I couldn't wait any longer to break the news to Terr. It was so overdue, I felt guilty. I finally told him, on our way out of the Shard that first visit.

First he acted dumbfounded, which didn't surprise me. Then he looked away when we were on Tooley Street and got a faraway look, which I interpreted as a warm, grateful reaction, even though we had a difficult road ahead. I think he was quietly pleased without absorbing the longterm consequences. I regretted taking so long to tell him, but I didn't know myself, with a reasonable measure of assurance, until recently.

It must have been bittersweet for him. I'm going to be a Da again! But we have no modern maternity ward, or anyone at our disposal with medical expertise. At all. We hardly have adequate tools, devices, or fresh water (although we'll be better prepared when the time comes).

In fact, civilization has been thrust back as far as the Middle Ages or beyond; just after the Black Death. I have to carry a child into this darkness, this gaping maw of the perilous unknown.

Delivering a child is a difficult event *with* nurse midwives and a physician. We have neither. I can only imagine what it's going to be like.

I guess I'm being overly optimistic and in denial about how hard the next 4.5 months are going to be. Right now, all I have is Terr and Hepburn, the latter providing warmth and the courage of companionship, at most.

But I'm not scared. I'm Emma Wallace Blair, dammit! It's as simple as that: I have an unerring confidence that this child can be born, and delivered with reasonable health, under the circumstances.

I don't really think about what's going to happen to me during childbirth. It's a bloody scary scenario to put your mind through. Good thing I haven't had a child yet or witnessed childbirth. Ignorance is bliss.

I have Terr. He's uncommonly efficient in a variety of circumstances, so who knows what he can offer when the time arrives? I have confidence in him nonetheless.

Our interactions with Greta and her depleted sanctuary of human-race savers didn't last long. We left the first day after meeting them in the glass tower, and got back to Hepburn, who was going crazy alone inside the train. We gave her a long walk and a decent meal.

I envy her, in a way. She has a dog's way of breaking everything down to its simplest terms.

Be loyal to your overseers. Only really think about the next

155

hour. Eat, drink, pee, poo, wag tail, fetch, sleep. She's been very attentive to me as I get more and more pregnant, as in visibly so. She follows me around more than ever, nuzzling me and licking my hand. A dog knows. More universal understanding emanating from Hepburn.

She also remembers that I saved her. We have a bond for life.

The recovery of the Harley motorcycle upset our plans somewhat. Due to the bicycles, which got left near the Shard. We came back twice on the Harley to fetch the bikes. Then I would ride back to the train, with the motorcycle driving slowly nearby. At some point, Terr will teach me how to drive the motorcycle.

Each time we came back to get a bicycle, we called in on Greta and her gang. Got a meal out of it. I felt like I was only stopping in out of guilt, given that they seemed the only other healthy humans in London.

I outlined my theory about H7N11, so they could pass it on to the Australians and Norwegians, if they ever connected again. Greta and Colin kept trying to sell the Shard on us, more intensely each visit. They wanted us to join the commune, but I didn't see the point, and distrusted them by instinct. I always trust my gut.

Terr then overheard a conversation Colin was having with Greta when I wasn't in the room. Terr had been tinkering with their communications equipment. I was in the bathroom. When he returned, this is what he overheard...

They were talking about being present for my delivery in four months or so, with word choices and weird tones suggesting the event must involve something akin to the birth of the baby Jesus. A mystical and enraptured moment for humanity, not merely a profound ordeal for me.

Then what Colin said next was the utter deal-breaker, evidence that they were twisted and off their rockers. He suggested that I should be impregnated again, ASAP after the baby's birth. And that the father should be someone other than Terr! Like himself!

That was it for me! Those control freaks were harboring some kind of eugenics-based sperm-donor fantasy.

Terr took me by the arm and we abruptly left the Shard, never to return. Back to the train at King's Cross, we settled in, me nurturing a growing belly. The next looming decision was whether we were going to stick with the train for the duration of my pregnancy. Our gut instincts told us: stay in the known familiar place, until the kid is born, then maybe we can look for something more.

Oddly bourgeois of me given our circumstances. "We need a bigger place, dear."

Terr still has a fondness for his home area of Farnborough, which has a lot more countryside, big empty houses, and undoubtedly, many more places we can scavenge at.

I figure we have about two months to decide, when I enter my third and final trimester.

CHAPTER 40: 60 DAYS LATER; LATE FALL, 2028

The chorus of howling and yipping begins every night around 2 AM. It's hard to tell how many of them there are, but it creates an unholy din. We can't go outside at night unarmed anymore. It's only Terr now, if ever.

I don't know whether the wild dogs are infected, because I've never seen a specimen. If they are, if H7N11 can in fact use canines as hosts, then the packs would be even more dangerous and unpredictable.

Now starting to waddle about the train yard, I'm too scared to venture beyond King's Cross. I feel the kicking a lot. Hormones are raging. Terr deals with wildly swinging moods with aplomb, or he simply ignores me and leaves to find something to do around the train.

Pregnant, I certainly have no problems weighing nine to ten stone.

The train has one mirror in the bathroom. I look at myself topless. My quite-a-bit-larger breasts and the lowish hanging tummy, the size of a deflated volleyball. That means it's supposed to be a boy, but I know that's an old wive's tale.

Hepburn, who sleeps beside me every night, hears the howling before I do. She barks back, and I try to silence her, because I don't want to alert the wild dogs to our exact location, which they undoubtedly know anyways by scent.

I figure they have plenty of food sources without having to chase us down–rats, mice, rabbits, keeled over reivers–but that thought won't ease my angst. King's Cross suddenly isn't all that safe anymore.

Dated: November 3, 2028

I haven't written in the journal lately, given what we've gone through.

I'm almost seven months pregnant now. Roughly eight weeks to the big day. We're down to five gallons of water, two bags of rice, 12 cans of soup, and a ziplocked bag of ten matchbooks. I shuffle about with about half of my usual speed and energy.

Hepburn got out five days ago. It's happened a few times before, but she's been really easy to catch. Not this time. She vanished into the surrounding neighborhood, not answering our frantic calls. I wept profoundly, afraid we'd lost her.

I called and called for her from the King's Cross courtyard, played high notes on my pipe. Nothing. Then I did something that I now realize was selfish: I made Terr go looking for her. Not for long, but covering five square blocks. The unexpected outcome was entirely my fault.

"She'll come back. Just give it time," he said.

"She won't, I know it. This feels different. I'm afraid she's trapped, maybe cornered, somewhere. There's no escape and..." I choked up.

"You and your animal rescue league," he said with obvious impatience. But he couldn't say "no." I was sure of that, given my condition and pathetic pleas.

"You almost got yourself drowned in Loch Ness the last time. Hell, Hepburn's better off than we are. She's more mobile. She can run faster, longer, and find food anywhere."

I turned away to the windows of the train, the silence of the sepulchral, unused platforms. Tears streamed down my face; I was distraught, inconsolable, as if I can't have the baby without Hepburn present.

"Oh, alright," Terr said with resignation. He *is* the father of my child, after all. He grabbed his shotgun and exited to the courtyard, where the motorcycle was parked. I started to follow. He barked over his shoulder, "You stay here. For God sakes, don't move or try to follow me."

I heard the motorcycle's loud cough and the ignition kicked in and sputtered, black condensation dripping from the exhaust pipe. It was a deafening sound for this emptied out London neighborhood. The shotgun was slung over his shoulder as he pulled away on the Harley.

I waited outside the train, pacing, literally wringing and knitting my hands.

I couldn't stand the fact that I would have to wait, out of earshot.

Two hours went by, seemed like eight. I sat on the stairs leading up into the passenger car and cried into my hands. Finally, I heard the motorcycle. I got up and did a fast-waddle to the courtyard. I found the motorcycle laying on its side. Terr lay beside it, bleeding from his neck, hands, and other places.

160

Hepburn stood above him, tail slowly wagging. Terr had returned, grievously injured, with Hepburn straddling the space between Terr and the handlebars.

When I went over to Terr, he was in the fetal position with a hand covering his face. He wasn't moving. Eyes closed. I could detect his chest moving up and down like the breast of a stunned bird, but that was it.

I'm a pregnant woman with a dog marooned in a blighted city. The thought plagued me: I'm doomed without Terr.

CHAPTER 41

I'd have to surrender to the care of the Shard cult, and whatever plans they had for me. Sobbing convulsively, I gingerly kneel down next to him, go cross-legged, and feel like a far more helpless chick.

His body doesn't have too many places where it isn't mauled.

"Terr, can you hear me? Oh dear boy, what have they done to you?" I comb the hair out of his eyes, my fingers coming away with a warm smear of his dark blood.

His eyes blink, close again. He seems to be nursing a multitude of pain points, and reluctant to come out of a semi state of consciousness. After a long pause: "The bloody dogs…they drug me off the bike…I got off one shot…"

Another pause that takes forever, then: "I'm done."

"No, you're not. Get up and move. We have to get inside, so I can disinfect you. If you can talk, you can move."

He shifts his left leg, as though to flex the knee. Then he gives up and it slumps back to the pavement. He has jagged tears and blood stains on his trousers. I take out a kerchief and wiped more of the blood off his face, only managing to smear it on the collar of a shirt.

He has several nasty lacerations, bite marks on hands and forearms where he'd fought them off. I was afraid of rabies, and H7N11.

He blinks again and groans, as much in response to my crying and cajoling, as to his pain, which had to have radiated from dozens of places.

"Load the gun…with another shell." He motions feebly to a front trouser pocket. I fish a red cylindrical 12-gauge round out of it. He wrestles out of the shotgun, which was strapped around his shoulder, then scrapes it across the pavement toward me.

"What am I supposed to do with that?"

"Load it," he whispers. "Then shoot the bloody bastards. If they come back."

"I can't do that!"

"You might have to…"

With a barely perceptible nod, he says, "go on, take it."

With some fumbling around and him pointing–he had demonstrated how to do this before but I haven't much practice–I load the spare shell into it.

Then I strap the weapon around my own shoulder, careful not to nudge, with the hardwood stock, my prominent, tender abdomen. The rifle feels three times as heavy as its seven pounds. I'm flagging, as if I could promptly pitch forward onto my face.

He's still stationary. Now I'm pissed. "C'mon you wuss!" I snap. "I'm carrying at least two stone or 28 pounds extra, plus

163

this shotgun. But I'm still willing to drag you back to the passenger car in this state. You have to help me!"

He rolls his eyeballs in exasperation. Then he turns onto his left side, and with my urging, struggles to a sitting position.

"That's a good lad." I plant a kiss on the top of his head, which seems to break his resistance, his desire to lick his wounds and stay put. The kiss pleasantly surprises me; we seldom have had intimacy since I realized I was pregnant. But this momentary tender contact, given the circumstances, benefits both of us.

We've certainly had no deep kissing and heavy petting for months, I think. Romance always takes a back seat to survival: eating, drinking, and avoiding infected marauders.

Terr struggles mightily to his feet. It's his second wind. Hepburn has been waiting patiently, but now she runs to the entrance of the King's Cross station, sensing we're finally going home.

Terr leans heavily on my left shoulder, I say, "follow Hepburn."

Breathing in rasps, he limps on mostly one leg. Now I'm dragging another weight across the flagstones; baby, rifle, wounded man who weighs well over 12 stone, even on our lean diet.

"Use the other leg. I'm going to drop you!" Hepburn stops and stands at the entrance to King's Cross station, barking furiously at something in the streets behind us.

Make it only be an aimless tottering reiver, I think to myself.

The sunlight, which had blazed over the rooftops across Pancras Road, dims into shadows. I hold tightly to Terr as we make laborious progress toward the entrance, then I dart a glance behind me.

At least six coywolves, or coyote/wolf hybrids, stand like statues on Pancras Road, noses in the air. They're about 70 pounds, and all the same light shade of grey.

Shit! I make a fast calculation, even while terrified–five yards to the entrance then shut the door. But no, how can I do that? That door was automatic and now it's jammed!

Terr realizes what's happening and the fate that awaits both of us. He drags himself across the flagstones, then hurls himself inside the entrance to King's Cross Station, where Hepburn still barks madly.

I sense more like a shift in the wind. The coywolves make a move. Terr screams, "save yourself Emma!"

CHAPTER 42

The coywolves approach in a vee formation, led by an alpha male with a light grey coat and penetrating, ghoulish white eyes. I remember the stampeding reivers in Edinburgh, Terr standing at the entrance to Waverley Station brandishing the shotgun.

An eager whimpering accompanies their charge. I hear their claws on the pavement.

"For Chrissakes, let'em have it!" Terr bellows from just inside the station. I bring the barrel up, the stock resting on my righthand rib cage, one hand on the trigger, the other clutching the forestock.

A trickle, then a stiffer flow, wets the inside of my right leg. I sense two hearts beating madly. My mouth has gone sandpapery dry.

Somehow I'm detached from and uncaring of the wetness on my leg. In times of acute danger, we have a built-in mechanism for favoring some priorities (life and limb) over others (vanity, pride, creature comforts). It only occurs to me later that the stress could have broken my water.

I level the barrel, siting the alpha dog. I push the forestock beneath the barrel forward and back and with a greasy metallic snap, chambering the first round.

The roar of the weapon echoes off empty building facades. The kick knocks me backwards. The air is acrid with hot cordite.

I pivot my body to the left, push the forestock forward and back. It already feels more natural...*ker-chunk!* Another round chambered. I pull the trigger and a loud crack issues. The back of the rifle kicks painfully in my side.

The lethal buckshot sprays against two more coywolves. They drop muzzles first, skid, and leave bloodstains on the pavement.

I stumble backwards blindly, one hand on my abdomen by instinct, barely staying on my feet, my mouth dry as bone and the black smoke singeing my eyes. At the periphery, I watch a snarling Hepburn hit the coywolf on our right flank.

A furious admixture ensues: bared teeth, nails, airborne spit. A violent ball of snarling, brawling fur. I hear the yelps from bites and the scratching of claws on flagstones.

Three of the coywolves lie still like wet slabs of red meat. I swing the gun around at Hepburn's assailant. *Ker-chunk!* goes the forestock. Then I fire at its fleeing hindquarters.

I'm hit by a wave of dizziness and nausea. Swaying on my feet, I drop the gun to the stones with a dull clatter. Then I bend over, turn my head slightly, and barf the sparse contents of my stomach onto the ground, coughing and sobbing.

It's been a long day.

CHAPTER 43

Dated: November 8, 2028

That first night, after we got back into the train, we did some cursory bandaging. I cleansed the wounds with a little water–I didn't have much–and propylene glycol. The rubbing alcohol stings and should have elicited complaints from Terr and Hepburn, but didn't. They bravely gutted through it, bless their hearts.

Through the next hour, I figured out that my companions weren't going to die. Then I summarily passed out and we all slept well into the next day.

Both man and dog were badly mauled, but were going to pull through.

Hepburn, courageous for protecting my right flank against the attack, was over-matched and fared far worse in the fight with the coywolf, which ended up getting shot in the arse as it

*fled. Hepburn crawled into a corner of the passenger coach. I
covered her with a blanket. She let me cleanse and tie gauze
onto oozing wounds all over her body, her fur matted with
congealed blood.*

*I went from living day by day to hour by hour. I made soup,
mixed with rice. We could live on that, for a short time. It also
occurred to me that there were three dead coywolves lying in
the courtyard outside of King's Cross.*

Those aren't merely corpses. That's potential food.

*But when I waddled out there with my axe, the flies had
already massed on the carcasses. I should have known; it had
already been more than 12 hours since I shot them. They would
have had to be butchered right away, and were probably too
lean regardless. Ce la vie.*

*I walk around all the time now with my hand on my
abdomen, as if I was stroking and reassuring the child. I was,
in fact. That was awful acute stress we just went through, but I
still felt kicking, movement, even a lazy, liquid kind of turning
over at night. The wetness that coursed down my leg during the
fight was fear pee, not birthing water. Thank God.*

*More notches for my cricket bat. I'm not gonna split hairs;
it counts if I use a shotgun. I held nothing against those
coywolves, just trying to survive as they may. But I had an
infant and myself to protect.*

*Terr makes a slow but steady recovery. Nothing seems
infected, so far. He's had no fever. The wounds aren't pussy or
smelling. No stitches needed. Good thing, because that's not
one of the skills I've required. I could do it, if I have to, with
our sewing kit.*

*Terr is drawn, pallid, beaten. He's lost a lot of blood and
might have had certain muscles and tendons lacerated or
punctured. His mobility is limited.*

We've got no pain killers beyond salvaged old ibuprofen and the Scotch we pilfered from the Cullin Hills hotel and another place in the Kyle of Lochalsh. Never a 25-year-old. I used 8-year-olds, which were fine medicinally, minus the sting of having squandered good Scotch on disinfecting wounds.

I often write of the deprivations and sacrifices of survival life. There are also small to large pleasures, like booze and sex, that you don't have to deny yourself.

Terr needs several days to recuperate, that's for sure. He looks like a wounded soldier left on a crude surgical table in a Civil War-era tent.

We have to find food and water again. As the old adage goes: three weeks without food (in our present states, we would never survive a fast like that…), and three days without water, is all you got.

It's all on me this time, searching for the water.

CHAPTER 44

I left the next morning. I had a backpack and as many empty jugs for water as I could stuff into it. I took the handgun, safety on. God forbid the thing goes off by accident, with me being pregnant. I put it in a side pocket of my baggy pants.

The axe I bungeed to the outside of the backpack. I took it along more as a tool; I might have to chop my way into a cabinet or some other storage container to get the water, and potentially, food.

I wasn't planning to just randomly search the neighborhoods off Pancras Road near the train station. I had a plan. Two shops nearby; only them. I have to minimize my exposure on the streets. Only during the morning hours, when everything seems quieter.

The coywolves aren't about, even though I read once that wolves can wake up every two hours. Sounds like me lately.

It's a beautiful morning, I idly note, to boost my morale.

The first thing I do if I find water is guzzle to my heart's content. Better to carry water inside yourself, than lug all of it with my sore back and arms.

If you keep this up, you're going to miscarry... This thought doesn't plague me anymore, like it used to. I've already come to terms with a life fraught with danger and uncertainty. Now I have live cargo along for the ride. That's the only difference. It's sink or swim.

Walking with purpose under the sun feels incongruously good, considering the hazards I'm exposed to and the state of my companions. The sleep did me good. This kid inside me, if anything, will inherit wanderlust; an innate ability to cover long distances as needed. That's all I've been doing while pregnant: wandering, scavenging, and fighting.

I reach the first shop. It's burned and busted, smelling of damp wood ash and rotten food. Probably a propane explosion. Doesn't look promising. Savvy about these things, I won't waste a minute sifting through these ruins.

I move along on the sunny sidewalk to the next shop off of Pancras. It's across the street, kitty corner to the burned one, and crossing over is where I find a thin stream, flowing down the soiled gutter. It's from a broken main, most likely. Yes! I'm shocked that a reservoir still exists for a broken pipe to draw from. I eagerly follow the flow upstream, like a refugee in search of an oasis.

I walk Pancras Road to a smaller intersecting street; the stream swings around from an uphill contour of the road.

The sun blazes off a cluster of London's empty glass monoliths, which resemble a lost civilization I've only recently stumbled upon. The sky is flawless, minus any contrails. I hear only the wind, and a faint trickle from the flow at my feet.

Now my hand rests alternately on my abdomen and the

handgun. The metal weight knocks against the side of my leg. The safety is still on. From the gutted apartment houses and storefronts drifts an fetid aftermath of fires and the catastrophic pandemic: rotting food, animal waste, bodies.

My sense of smell is so acute now. I think I recognize the odor of wet fur that often wafts from Hepburn.

Then just as quickly, the road's scent shifts to floral, drifting from untended but thriving parks in Westminster.

Still no reivers, ambulatory or prone. I pray the coywolves have scattered to the wind. I know that's wishful thinking. We didn't shoot up the only pack in town.

The stream winds its way through mud, oil, and gutter debris. The flow is faster, I feel I'm near its source. A cracked pipe with water bubbling up through the fissures is what I imagine. I'll take it; the Thames as a source or not.

Around the corner I find a busted hydrant. Clear water gushes and foams onto the sidewalk. But standing at the foot of the hydrant are two gray coywolves, heads down, about to lap up the water that's spilled on the street.

Shit...again! I backpedal, slowly, hoping they haven't detected me.

One looks up, ears twitching, cold glaring eyes with luminous white irises. I'm not 30 yards distant. The other one looks up. Now they're both staring at me. Sizing me up. It's me or a drink.

I slowly move my hand to the side pocket where the handgun is stored. I fumble around for it, can't find the handgrip. I need time to take the safety off; both our hearts start racing again, me and the tike's. I'm screwing up, the barrel of the gun is wadded up in my trousers.

This time, I have no pee to involuntarily release.

Backpack down, handgun finally out, hands trembling,

safety off. I raise the shaking barrel. I can feel my seven-month-old's heart beat like a hummingbird's.

I stiffly hold the beretta out in front and sight the first coywolf.

He takes a few drunken, myopic steps in my direction. Then he oddly turns and makes a full circle. He barks, like a hiccup, apparently at nothing. The other one wanders away from the hydrant aimlessly into the middle of the road.

The predator who'd made a half hearted move in my direction summarily collapses onto his side. The tongue lolls out. Eyes still stare, as though seeking a destination just out of reach. The other one, moments later, keels over in the middle of the road, as if knifed in the heart.

They didn't look starved, shot, or otherwise wounded; they looked sick.

I wondered about the water.

CHAPTER 45

I never saw them drink from it. And they both looked generally haggard and sickly.

I don't believe there is anything wrong with this water, flowing clear out of the hydrant. I don't even think it's risky. I've been drinking London's water, from residential and restaurant kitchens, whenever I can find it.

I remove the jugs from the backpack and fill them at the hydrant. No more coywolves, from what I can see. The two still appear dead as nails. I tip a jug up and guzzle greedily, standing there alone in the street, the water spilling down both cheeks.

It tastes cool and relatively clear. I don't detect any floating solids or sour or bitter tastes. Neither does it taste like Thames water, which would be gritty and rust-colored.

The backpack is stuffed to the gills with heavy water jugs. It weighs a ton, but I have to carry it. I resigned myself to that task long ago.

I have an overwhelming desire to piss. It's out of relief, not fear, that I squat in the open, staying vigilant, scanning both ends of the Camley Street neighborhood. A puddle forms beneath me. Then, still faintly embarrassed out of old habits and mores, I stand and zip up my pants.

The backpack must weigh 40 pounds now or three stone. It's a huge effort to hoist it to my back. *Don't get a hernia! Don't tear an abdominal muscle or do anything that will lead to a miscarry!*

Those internal voices plague me. At the same time, however, I'm proud of my efforts. I will simply take what comes, with my child. We all need water. I'm the only one who can fetch and tote it right now. I have no choice, and that realization is almost calming.

Including the child, the amniotic fluid, and my extra pregnancy weight, I might be hoisting 60 extra pounds or more than four stone.

I waddle Camley to Pancras Road. It quickly becomes a death march. I'm conscious of the possibility of dizziness and passing out. One foot falls heavily in front of the other. My breath is labored. I move forward inexorably.

I note the hydrant location on Camley–I'll return here for more water. I only go one block, before I have to stop every other step, as if I'm climbing a steep mountain. Finally, I recognize the train station facade, the courtyard, like a haunting mirage. Abject fatigue is like a dream state. It begins raining, a light patter on the sidewalk. I crawl along the edge of the sidewalk near the looming facades of vacant buildings, windows like black eyes.

I enter the courtyard in front of King's Cross, feeling like I'm going to pitch forward disastrously. I rigidly hold onto myself; avoiding a fall that would have many very bad consequences.

Terr waits for me outside. It's the first time he's been any distance off the train. He approaches me with an uncertainty that seems like he's trying out his legs the first time, to see if they work. This unsteadiness is incongruous with the still visible bulk and heft of his body.

He sits down on the bench near me. It's under a tree, protected from the drizzle. For me, the rain is refreshing, reviving.

"Thanks for fetching the water. You're doing everything," he says with a mild guilt.

"No worries." I unhitch the backpack, then let it drop off my back onto the bench, sensing the immense release of a burden. I sit down next to him, utterly knackered. I breath deeply, feeling my heart rate, then the infant's, recover somewhat.

Survival for another hour, accomplished. "There's a lot of water where I found it. A broken hydrant. Camley Street." He raises an eyebrow, impressed.

"I'll go next time."

"Maybe. You didn't have to wait for me in the rain, though I appreciate it."

"I can't stand solitude anymore, just me and the dog. It drives me bonkers. I have to move, anyhow."

"What about the Kyle? You were alone, not even a dog."

"That was different. I thought I was alone in the world, living in me own head. How's the child?"

He said that with a furrowed brow. Given the strenuous pregnancy, the rough ride this kid has had, I understand the concern.

"The child's moving. And no longer thirsty, I hope. I just

drank about a gallon, before I filled up six jugs. Here. Have one." I reach towards the backpack, but he gently pushes the arm away. He wants to do it himself.

He pulls a jug out of the pack, twists the top off, sips, puts it down.

I laugh, thinking of my own tender, distended jugs, already brimming with milk. Actually, something called colostrum. They used to be perky, and only noticeable that way, under sweaters and light shirts.

I take his hand and thoughtfully place it on my abdomen. The wind swirls around the wet courtyard like a gentle third companion.

"Do you feel that? The kick? The little nudge?"

"Wow," he says, a wide, toothy grin breaking the strain of his face. Then he takes on a thoughtful look.

"What do you want to call her?"

"Her?"

"Ha." He shakes his head, faintly chastened.

"Freudian slip. You want a girl. Funny, most men want boys."

"I didn't mean anything by that. Not like that old bitch Greta, and her sod boyfriend, and all that bollocks about using you to repopulate the world. It was a slip of the tongue."

"No offense taken."

I take his hand off my stomach, place it on his knee, leave my hand there.

"What do you want to name him, or her?" he asks.

"I don't know. Haven't really given it enough thought." I haven't had the luxury of empty time to think of it, to be honest. Only idle thoughts and fantasies here and there. "Maybe after your children. You had a boy and a girl, right?"

Darkness suddenly colors his face. "No. I want to leave

them be." He looks away toward some trees cloaked in well watered green leaves. Existing in their glorious isolation, it's as though the hardwoods of London inhabited a different realm than the one ravaged by a pandemic.

He finally says: "How 'bout I think of a boy's name, you think of a girl's?"

"Why not the opposite? I'll think of a boy's, you think of a girl's. Jazz it up a bit." The conversation makes me temporarily forget about coywolves, exhaustion, thirst, pregnancy…everything.

"It's a deal."

I did have a boy's name in mind, probably conjured up in the minutes before sleep. "How about Erik Blair Winslow."

"It has a ring."

I felt relaxed. We paused. The rain had stopped. A clean, sterile smell rose from the concrete. Sunlight filtered through the leaves.

We seemed surrounded by an ocean of normalcy, like an incoming tide.

CHAPTER 46

"Rebecca," he said, four fingers lightly tapping his leg. "Rebecca Wellington Blair."

"Why Wellington? No Winslow?"

"Don't care about my surname, in that way. Besides, Wellington has a flair, don't you think? A certain distinction. That statue of 'im we saw in Edinburgh."

"The red construction cone on his head…"

"Yet he was still the nobleman, up there on his horse. His high horse…the sword at his side…" He changed the subject. "I think I'll take the water back to the train."

"You sure?"

He picked the pack up with one crooked, burly arm and slung it over his shoulder. "Piece of cake."

He began to walk back slowly toward the dim platform.

"I like the name," I called after him.

"So do I."

Dated: November 20, 2028

Just short of running out of food, Terr was able to rally and accompany me on scavenges. His wounds had healed reasonably well. So had Hepburn's. They both walked with limps.

We'd run out of both weed and CBD oil, as expected. It was going to take a concerted search of London dispensaries and homes to find any more. I wasn't going to take any with the child in me anyways, but Terr felt their absence. I was still convinced that we needed CBD and its derivatives to stay well.

I'm well into the third trimester. I take walks in the sun with the ever present hand on the abdomen and a glassy look (so's Terr remarks on it), which amounts to a slice of maternal heaven. If it wasn't for the fact that I live in a world ravaged by a pandemic.

So be it. I think we've all done damn well so far at this survival game. Almost everyone is dead or staggering around with poisoned minds, except for us.

Terr hunts: squirrels, rabbits, seabirds, frogs from the teeming ponds in the parks (boiled or grilled, eat the legs, a French delicacy). To that we add whatever we can scavenge: crackers, peanut butter, jam, rice and beans, wild apples, mint leaves and parsley (not filling but nutritious), protein powder, and the last of the powdered milk we rescued from the farm in Skye.

The barebones calories I was still on guaranteed I wouldn't have a fat child. I took the salvaged multivitamins, and I ate bowls of protein powder mixed with water. It's a tasteless porridge that otherwise gave both of us a minimum of the protein we needed.

Maybe it's an Erik who's getting that protein hit too. I have

181

a mild inkling I'm carrying a boy.

Terr took the motorcycle out this morning to fetch food. The bike is way handier than walking (especially at my pace) and can cover hundreds of blocks on a single tank of gas. He had the backpack, and a plastic milk crate bungeed to the back of the bike.

I must admit to a little terror, as only three weeks before he'd gone out looking for Hepburn and came back in shreds. There're still coywolves out there, but the way those two coys expired before my eyes has gotten inside my head. Very suspicious.

Terr promised only to be gone an hour or two at most.

I've begun to take lessons on the bike myself, not that I'm ever going to ride it in this condition, but for later. It's rather easy to find car carcasses to siphon gas from, but that's Terr's domain, not mine. So for one brief shining moment, I anticipate we will have plenty water, food, and gas for a couple of weeks.

First an hour went by, then two.

Panic mode, an ominous foreboding, set in. He returned before sunset, just when I was becoming consumed by worry.

"Where the heck have you been?"

"Round and about."

"What do you mean?"

"I been around to the Thames and London Bridge. Found a pub. They had some beef jerky stuffed behind the bar. I found frozen fish and chips in an old fridge, melted but not spoiled. I got some blood sausage, too. So we can eat well tonight. Took me a while to get back though," he said sheepishly.

"Oh, well, no harm done. Let's get some beef jerky and salt the fish." I didn't think anything more of Terr's flighty bike trip, at least then.

He told me that Regent's Park had hundreds of bodies in it,

182

as though it was a common graveyard that people, like elephants, had migrated to. A sort of giant potter's field.

That's just the beginning of the explanation for where millions of sick Londoners have gone, because we haven't seen too many. Only a few reivers and corpses, here and there. Certainly the coywolves are living off them, and their population has increased many times over as a result.

When we relaxed and started eating, Terr got all quiet. Then he told me he'd completely forgotten the way home. Momentarily, he'd forgotten that we lived in a ScotRail train at King's Cross. He was looking for road signs for Farnborough, his old home. This freaked him out. Me too.

He mentioned a blow to the head he'd received when he toppled off his bike, trying to flee the coywolves. That seemed a good enough explanation. He doesn't wear a helmet, because he hasn't found one.

By God, I hope he's right. All I could think about was Will.

The next day, me riding on the back of the bike, on a food and pharmacy excursion south toward the Thames, we run into the first uninfected children I'd seen since before Skye and London. It was nothing short of bloody amazing.

CHAPTER 47

Three boys, all around ten. Looking soiled and scuffed and standing on Holborn near St. Bartholomew and the Blackfriars Bridge.

They stare at us as the motorcycle pulls up. One of them smiles and comes forward, the other two seem shy and hang back.

"Cool motorcycle!" the boy gushes. Terr pushes the kickstand down, cuts the engine, and straddles the bike, as I gingerly step off the back.

The kid glances up eagerly.

"Who are you?"

"Terr and Emma. And who might you be lad?"

"I'm Harry, and that's my brother and friend, Jack and Max. We live alone. We're superheroes."

"Is that right?" This cracks Terr's smile. Children, buoyant, living in this diseased wasteland. Who woulda thunk it.

"Pleased to meet you boys," I say, feeling a child's warmth surge up from somewhere around my pregnancy. It feels somewhat dream-like.

"Charmed, sure I am," Harry says, a soiled hand extended. I shake it. I don't care about the hygiene. Dirt is dirt and these kids are doing what kids do.

"Where are your parents?" I ask.

"They got the barmy fever and died. We don't much care anymore. We didn't even cry. We got our freedom."

"My." The other two boys shrug amiably, to show the positive side of losing your parents. I didn't think they were callous. I thought they were children, who learned how to survive.

"When's the last time you had a bath?"

They all have a shock of scissored hair, Harry's and Jack's a dirty blond, Max's a greasy black. Their clothes ill-fitting and torn in places: ordinary trousers with suspenders, button-down shirts, buttons missing. Torn and scuffed up sneakers.

I wanted to give them all a bath and seamstress their clothes. Maternal instinct rears its comely head.

"We go swimming...sometimes."

"Where do you all live?" I ask.

"The church," Harry proclaims. "You? Where do you hang your hats in London?"

"King's Cross Station. We live on a train."

"No kidding? Can we come see that sometime? Is it runnin'?"

"Your pullin' our leg, aren't yah?" Jack blurted out.

"Nah. You bet it's a workin' train," Terr says, with a paternal boast, like a dad bragging about an ancient sports accomplishment. "You can come, but I better see your tickets first, or your ScotRail pass, or I can't offer you a ride."

185

Harry's eager expression vanished, then Jack cried out: "You mug. He's just kidding. They don't take tickets anymore. The trains ain't runnin', at least 'til some grownups come back. Till then, they're all free!"

"He's right, Harry," Terr says, uneasily swinging a leg off the bike then brushing himself off.

Emboldened, Jack moves forward. One eye squints, the other doesn't.

"Say," he says to me. "You having twins there?"

"Gosh no. I don't think so. Feeding them? No, that would be difficult or impossible under the circumstances. I'm having *one*, for now. I'm giving it a welly, for one, only."

"Is it a lad," Harry says, eagerness reacquired. "Like us?"

"I don't know. Do you want to look? Maybe you can tell me." Being around children, and the devil-may-care courage they display, drains the tension and lifts my spirits. I begin to adjust the baggy shirt I'm wearing. Harry's jaw drops, as Jack and Max step forward.

I lift up the shirt, revealing the resplendent orb of my pregnancy.

"Can I touch?" Max asks, leaving his shyness behind.

"Of course you can. You can tell me if you feel a kick or a punch."

Max places his palm on my tight belly. "I felt it move! I did!" he declares wondrously.

"We saw a photo of tits," Harry says, distractedly and apropos of nothing. Jack and Max laugh, with Terr.

"Where?" Terr asks, with a sudden interest.

"Magazines..." Harry replies distantly.

Terr shoots a nonchalant glance at me.

"Some things never change."

"Well," I say. "You're not seeing mine. At least not now."

Jack turns to Max with a raised-eyebrow, "Oh wow" look. They both squinch their shoulders and giggle.

"You mean maybe later?" Harry quips sardonically.

"You are a sharpie aren't you? When women breast feed infants, they shan't be shy about doing it in the public eye. When the kid is hungry, she is hungry. You can't wait till you get home. Get my drift? You'd see them under no other circumstances."

"I'm savvy to that," Harry says, turning back to the motorcycle. "Maybe I can ride that."

"When you get older," Terr corrects. "Where's this church?"

"St. Paul's," Harry says. "Right down the road. That's home for me and my blokes."

"You live in *St. Paul's Cathedral?*"

"That's right. Only us. We're caretakers, like." Then he says, as if it was an afterthought: "Jesus Christ on the cross is looking over us."

"Apparently so," I say. I have to pee like you can't believe. "I'm going behind that wall over by the tree." Max looks at me, then at the tree, then back.

"We poo and pee in the graveyard, most of the time."

"Gross!" Jack yells, scowling at his mate.

"I'll steer clear of the graveyard, anyways," I say, as I waddle away. I pee well out of their eye-sight, then return to the little group standing under the trees. They resemble kids and teachers in a schoolyard, a scene that gives me escapist memories.

But only for the briefest moment can we let our guard down. While it still looks like London, in truth, it's a wild land of disease and feral beasts.

CHAPTER 48

"Where do you get your grub?" Terr asks, as I rejoin them, hand lingering on my abdomen, as if I was checking if the orb was still there.

Harry sweeps the neighborhood with his hand. "Everywhere. Sometimes it gets delivered to us."

"By who," I ask, playing along.

"Servants and livery," he replies, after a brief ponder. "We come from royalty you know, me and Jack."

"Then how come you ain't sippin' brandy over at Buckingham Palace?" Terr asks.

"We like St. Paul's better. The food is better. We like the digs. The size of the place fits us quite nice, I'd say."

"No seriously." I'm genuinely curious about the details. "Where does the food come from?"

Harry strides over to our backpack, which has some scavenged, and typically stale, bags of potato chips and pretzels poking out of the top. I eat almost anything we can scavenge these days; it goes without saying.

The pretzels provide some needed salt.

Harry has a brief look at our convenience market harvest. "Crap," he declares with disdain.

"What d'ya, have a personal chef?"

"Two," Harry says straight faced. "We're princes of England, aren't we? Except for Max, who's a Scottish bastard, descended from Robert the Bruce's strumpet."

"Watch what you say about the Scottish," I say sternly. "I'm from the north of Scotland."

Harry looks at me and blinks. "I've never been up there. That's my parents' fault. I've heard Edinburgh is…charming."

"When the gorse is in season, M'Lord. So what are you eating? Candy? Milk Duds? Chewing gum for desert?"

"We eat out of The Room," Jack says with blunt authority.

"We'll show you. Follow me," Harry says, turning up Rose Street and heading in the direction of the cathedral. "You're officially invited for dinner."

I look back at Terr and shrug. "Do we already have dinner plans, dearie?"

"If we do, it'll be beef jerky and stale peanut butter crackers. Again. So we might as well…"

Following Harry, Max, and Jack, we approach from the decorative front facade the still magnificent cathedral. It appears to take up an entire block and tops 350 feet high. It's retained its artistic magic, its holiness.

The dome, the three spires, the frontage made up of impressive columns and porticos, it seems to promise the return of normal, grand London. In that way, it's like a mirage.

We top a flight of stained marble steps and enter through a formal, oaken front door.

The church interior is cavernous and lit by shafts of mote-filled light. Harry takes us along the nave, rows of empty pews, shelves still manned with Hymn books. It's still a church smell, woody, moldy, but not malodorous.

The walls are covered with centuries-old artwork, lacquered images of Jesus drooped on the cross, mosaics of the Olde England countryside.

We walk up some steps and along the side of the chancel, which still has a set of gold-tinted chalices decorating an altar. The tables and chairs are covered by tattered red velvet. It seems like the boys have been lounging around on them.

I look up. The church balconies appear blindingly high. The ceiling dome is dizzying. St. Paul's is in remarkably good shape, and I suddenly understand why the three orphans took up residence there.

It's warm and hallowed and protected from the depredations of London's streets. No open doors, as far as I can see, for the coywolves or the reivers, should there actually be any lurking about.

The vast space, and its fancy archaic design, offers the reassurance of a past intact civilization. It feels like stepping into a history book.

St. Paul's survived two bombing hits during the Blitz in World War Two. One of the Nazi bombs embedded in the structure was timed to explode. But a Royal Engineer in demolition defused it, moved the explosive to a safe place, then blew it up. The bomb would have completely destroyed the cathedral. The engineer, whose name was Robert Davies, received the George Cross for his efforts, one of Britain's highest honors for bravery.

St. Paul's seems blessed in its history of surviving cataclysms. Maybe Harry, Max, and Jack had a sixth sense for choosing a reliable habitat, given the vast choices they had (though their decision-making certainly had to be rushed and made under great duress).

The chancel and altar are thick with an air of rectitude and antiquity.

Off to the side is a stairwell. We enter, follow the three boys. It's shadowy, lit only by the natural light streaming through tall stained-glass windows.

"We play the organ," Harry says offhandedly. "We figured out how to ring the church bell, but only once..."

Terr nods, then asks urgently, "Does the big front door lock? How do you keep out the daft bastards and the coywolves, the whole lot?"

Harry laughs at that one with his diffident confidence. "No one knows we're here. We have a secret royal society. You can be a member if you want, but you have to make an oath of blood. We use a sword. It's upstairs. It used to be King Arthur's!"

"Yeah, sure, I'm in. Who wouldn't want to be royalty?" Terr chuckles.

We go down stone steps two floors below. There are black soot stains on the brick walls and the stone floor is coarse and wet.

Harry stops in front of another ponderous wooden door. His eyes glint in the dim light. "This is The Room. It's secret. All dinners are served here."

Terr nods and pulls open the heavy door. It seems ridiculous in these church depths, with its ornate carving of a long lost king or knight embracing a sword and shield.

Harry strikes a match and lights torch lamps on each side of the inside of the entrance. The room is musty, like a basement. In the low flickering light, I see a round wooden table cluttered with plates and wooden mugs and strewn with delicious meaty tidbits, bowls of fruit, hunks of cheese, even a few decanters of church wine.

The shaft of dour hallway light hits the cornucopia like a dream. I lunge for the table, a starving animal, Terr close behind.

I'm only thinking of the deep maw of my stomach, distantly, the nutritional needs of my child. This ponderous, ever-present pregnancy is on my mind, not the mystery of the boys and their giant church.

They've led us to a magic reality.

CHAPTER 49

I quickly tear off a leg of fowl, smothered in crisp skin and containing still moist dark meat. I put it in my mouth and shamelessly bite and chew off pieces, until my cheeks are full. Harry laughs softly, almost paternalistically, in the near darkness.

Terr rakes a heavy wooden chair across the floor and dives into the food with both mitts. I feel terrible that we left Hepburn behind. It was only temporary. We'll bring back some food for her, for sure. Fresh meat. She just doesn't fit easily on the motorcycle.

I keep wolfing, filling a bottomless pit. We're eating ravenously with our hands, our fingers and the cheeks around our mouths slick with grease. We don't care. We haven't eaten like this since the Kyle of Lochalsh. I don't even bother to ask them where the food comes from.

"The Room," a magic store of delicacies, is good enough

for me.

We're sitting in a circle. Apples, grapes, cheddar and gouda cheeses, and the meat and bones of fowl, soft and mushy and dry in places but still delicious, litter the table in front of our chests. They even have a round loaf of stale olive bread and butter.

I tear spongy chunks off the loaf and scrape them across a gouged out slab of yellow butter sitting in a tin. No forks and knives need apply.

The boys are pleasantly amused to have guests. They only nibble, burp, laugh, make rotten food jokes, as if the feast is no big deal and London hasn't been decimated by a pandemic. It's as if, rather than immersed in hour to hour survival, we'd been invited to a lavish Olde England theme dinner.

Terr's chair scrapes across the stone floor as he pushes it away from the table, crumbs and scraps of food littering his place, his partly bearded face wet with food scraps.

"Bloody fine grub mates. I'm chuffed." He belches, unselfconsciously, glancing around with a half grin. "You must have looted half the best restaurants in London. How did we miss 'em? By the way, I'd like to try a bit of that wine."

"By all means," Harry says. "We've tried it, a lot. Me and the blokes, drinkin' together."

"All that's missing is the football." Terr reaches for a cut-glass decanter and fills a goblet with what looks like watered down Claret.

"Right. Watching football is a bit much to ask, isn't it? We *play* football though. We have two balls. We're taking them to Wembley, for a tournament. Upstairs. We kick them up on the pitch, outside," Harry explains proudly.

"That's bloody good." Terr holds his glass up to the warm light. He grunts in approval, then downs the glass in one quaff.

"Not bad."

"I think it tastes like vinegar," Jack says.

"Wine is wine, right now. The church wine is usually one of the cheapest. Diluted swill. A class above rotgut. This is my body, this is my blood, and the like…pass the bloody bottle." Terr refills his glass. He's getting a little drunk.

"Give me some more of that blood…"

"Blasphemy," Jack says, crossing himself.

"Once in a while we say grace," Max adds guiltily.

"I apologize for that," I mumble. "I mean, the gluttony and not saying grace. It's all very generous. Thank you thank you thank you."

"It's him, out there," Max says, and I don't exactly get his reference. "We owe it to Jesus. Our food and shelter. Not getting the barmy fever…"

Terr smiles. "Amen, lads." He crosses himself gleefully.

He's hard to watch, having a good drunken time. I want to quaff a glass myself. Take the edge off.

"One sip won't hurt, will it?" I guiltily pose to the table. I knew it was the equivalent of giving a sip of cheap belfry vintage to an infant. So it is.

I've been chaste up till now.

"I think me mum drank a pint 'a day with me onboard," Terr says blithely. "Probably two. G' head."

I pour not three fingers into a goblet. I sip it in a savory kind of way. It still goes to my head right away.

"Not bad. Not bad at all." Terr and I clink glasses in the warm light. It's almost like we're drinking 25-year-old Scotch again.

"Religion…" Terr says. "Got it crammed down my gullet as a kid. Not much good it did me. Did you hear the one about the guy in the sinking boat who prayed to God?"

"No," Harry says eagerly, with a half smile.

"Another boat comes by, and its captain yells out, 'Do you want to climb aboard my ship mate?' And the guy in the sinking boat says, 'No, I prayed to God to save me, and he will.'"

"'Suit yourself,' the captain says, and off he sails. The boat keeps sinking. A helicopter goes overhead. A rescuer yells down, 'Do you need help mate?'"

"'No. I prayed to God to save me and he will.' The helicopter flies away. Then a submarine pops up alongside the sinking boat. The skipper opens the hatch and yells, 'Do ya need help captain?' And the sinking-boat guy says 'Nah I prayed to God. He'll help me.' The submarine leaves, the guy's boat sinks, and he drowns."

Terr looks around mischievously. Everyone is quiet.

"So the captain who sunk his boat goes up to Heaven, through the Pearly Gates, and he says to God, 'I kept prayin' to yah and you didn't save me.' And God says, 'I sent you a ship, a helicopter, and a submarine. What else could I do?'"

Everyone laughs uproariously, Terr the most. It's a delightful moment, so un-pandemic.

I only drink three fingers and one more splash of the cheap altar boy's Claret. It feels wonderful, but laughter feels the best.

Boy, do I eat. A memorable feast. So does Terr. It's a marvel, a surreal stroke of luck, the way that food chunks and scraps litter the round wooden table.

"So you found yerselves a secret cache, huh?" Terr asks. "The priests, keepin' the food for themselves when the chips are down. What did I tell you about religion? Hypocritical bastards. Not that I don't love the meal…"

"Yeah, it's a secret cache. Still lots in there," Harry says.

"For our secret society."

"To the secret society," Terr toasts, quaffing again.

I get up uneasily, when it's time to return to Hepburn with our equivalent of a doggie bag: a canvas bag containing meat, bones, and cheese. Yes, Hepburn eats and likes cheese.

I waddle out of the room to the soft glow of the lamps, followed by our companions. I have a weary but warm and gratified buzz around me. The stairs seem steeper and longer than before.

The volume and variety of food have made the child more active than ever. Hand on my abdomen. Almost eight months. My. Top of the stairs. Clouds have covered the holy shafts of light in St. Paul's hollow-seeming nave.

Terr is jolly. He puts his arm around me and kisses me cheek.

We bid a farewell to the boys at the lumbering ponderous door to St. Paul's. We fully expect to return the next day with Hepburn.

I thought it was his consumption of the wine. That certainly contributed to it, but I have to show Terr all the way to the motorcycle. I have to remind him that we lived at King's Cross, not far from the cathedral. He looks at me blankly. The man who was bitten and torn by coywolves.

"How do you feel?" I ask, distressed with total Mum's paranoia.

"Like a happy high. Hardly pissed…bottles away from that."

"Okay."

He looks at me with a flushed face, and his eyes go glassy and narrow. A familiar film of bewilderment overtakes them. He gets quiet for a minute, sitting on his bike, me holding him around the waste.

He makes the words "King's Cross Station Euston Street" with his lips, as though the words derive from a foreign language.

He's scaring the daylights out of me.

CHAPTER 50

"I can't bloody remember my own Mum's name! My kids'!"

"Francis and Wendy. Your wife, Maggie."

"Okay, I can recall that, after a reminder!" he says mordantly.

"Tell me this then: what's the train route we took from Skye?" I do this to reassure him.

"East to Inverness. South to Perth, and the Aberdeen line, through Edinburgh."

"And…?"

"South to York, and London's King's Cross."

"See? You've got lots of memory left."

"The train lines are in my blood."

"I forget shit all the time," I say, exaggerating somewhat. "I forgot what month it was. And I'm not even sick. I had to look at my journal."

We're back in the train in King's Cross. Hepburn sits at my feet, being fed scraps from the church. She chews each morsel in record time, watching Terr with a kind of silent devotion.

I go on: "I'm forgetting my friend's names over the years. Look, it's been a while and we're under tremendous stress. In a way, we're lucky to be alive..."

"Lucky," he says, now subdued. "Luck is luck because it hasn't run out yet."

"It's getting dark. It's been a long day. We have a lot of food and drink in our bellies. As the old saying goes, you'll feel better in the morning."

"I did have a lot of wine," he says thoughtfully.

I walk Hepburn, no farther than the courtyard. I'm feeling nervous, tense. I make Hepburn sit and I pet her, to acquire that warmth flowing through me. We don't even have to talk about it. Terr thinks he's getting H7N11. That thought I can't dislodge.

I try to rationalize the counter argument. It's a solid one. H7N11 moves fast. He was bitten more than two weeks ago. I think of the stumbling, shambling coywolves by the gushing hydrant, which we have to revisit tomorrow.

Terr will drive me over there. It will take our minds off this.

Dated: December 16, 2028

I wake up this morning with lower abdominal pain. I wonder if the kid's foot, or the shoulder, is in the right place. I don't know if anything is in the right position, frankly. Look what I *haven't* had, which every modern pregnant woman undergoes: ultrasounds, regular checkups–poking and prodding, amniocentesis, the whole nine yards. I've been

*vertical and horizontal and pouring food down and monitoring
what comes out the other end. Not much else.*

*I've been feeling the kicks and the punches. I've been
talking and singing to this child, floating in its bath of 98.6
degree fluid and clueless of the fatal dangers that lurk outside
of me.*

*To be done with it. That's mostly what I'm thinking. 31
days, if he or she comes out on time.*

*I've slept well, nonetheless. Terr told me he has a slight
hangover, but nothing more. Something about his tone, a kindly
weariness, makes me think he's hiding something. Like the
grandfather who knows he has a mortal illness, but lives his
days in graceful kind words and tells no one.*

*To help relax, I read the Yeats poem A Prayer For My
Daughter:*

> *Once more the storm is howling, and half hid*
> *Under this cradle-hood and cover lid*
> *My child sleeps on...*

> *May she be granted beauty but not*
> *Beauty to make a stranger's eye distraught*
> *Or hers before a looking glass...*

Yes, I'm thinking it's a she...

*We drive slowly over to the same place with the hydrant,
which seems so close on a motorcycle. Fill the water jugs. The
gush is about a third of what it was before. We drink our fill.
The coywolf corpses are gone; I don't bother to speculate.*

*The day goes quickly with our chores: Get water, light fire,
prepare food, chat briefly about returning to St. Paul's
Cathedral, which is only one and three quarters miles walking
distance away. Walk Hepburn again, a little longer, beyond the*

courtyard, now seeming windswept and ominous as Winter comes on.

Terr is much much quieter, which makes me nervous. I ask him for a joke; he comes up empty. I ask him again how he feels. Okay. Then he shocks me by sitting me down at the end of the day for a talk.

I keep remembering: it's been several weeks since we've had any weed or CBD oil. Those coywolves at the end there were sick. Some debilitating virus, or autoimmune condition. I'm haunted by these thoughts.

I don't know what I will do if I lose Terr. I'm at least eight months pregnant with his child. I just don't know.

CHAPTER 51

"Your name is Emma Blair. This is Hepburn," he mumbles, petting the dog. We're sitting in the courtyard in a cold sun that crests a cloud like a flaming crown. A slight breeze musses up his thinning hair.

I reach out and part it to the side, brushing his forehead. It's warm. We otherwise have thicker layers on, me a baggy sweatshirt topped by a blanket.

"We're sitting in King's Cross, living out of a passenger train. I don't remember much else. I got this feeling like the slate's been erased."

"You remember the Kyle Of Lochalsh. The life you built there."

"Vaguely. Look..." He holds out his hand and it's trembling noticeably. "I've been sweatin' this morning, from the brow. I haven't gotten sick like that, since it happened. Just head colds...I can't remember, my mum or me da! I don't

203

remember their faces! Their names!"

"I hardly remember mine. You probably have a touch. It's a miracle we don't get sick more often. Just...take the day off. You know how the mind plays tricks on you. You took a pill?"

I meant one of our stale ibuprofens. "Yeah, two."

"So then, why don't you sleep. I'm going to walk Hepburn."

He stands up unsteadily, turns, and shuffles back toward the entrance to the train station. I have to admit to myself; he's a different Terr, at least in the last 48 hours. The swagger and bravado, almost all gone. He's a sick, a limited person.

As he walks away, Hepburn issues two clipped barks in his wake, as if Terr was a faintly threatening stranger to her.

Dated: December 19, 2028

I've never been an overly sentimental person. Neither was Terr, from what I've seen. I woke up this morning and only noted offhand we were five days before Christmas.

I found a note from Terr. Shakily scrawled. Laid on the seat next to mine. Must have left at four, when he knows I sleep the deepest. Or 4:30. It said:

Dear Emma,

I left early this morning. Packed a few things. I wanted to tell you but I didn't want you to stop me. I'm sicker. I've got the dreaded sickness, in the head. We know there's no cure. Don't think of it as me giving up. But I don't want to be helpless with you and the baby around.

I won't turn into one of those daft bastards! I won't become a danger to you and the child! I won't! I bloody won't allow it!

I left all the food and water for you. The pistol. Here's what you should do today. Pack up some things and go over to the boys at St. Paul's. Between the three of them, they can help

204

take care of you and the baby. Not me.

The motorcycle is yours. Be careful with it. If you want to say goodbye, go to the Tower Bridge at 10:30 AM, if you're up. I've found a dinghy down there…

'There's no way I'm going to let him go!' I'm thinking. So I close up Hepburn in the train and waddle over to the motorcycle. It's about 9:30 am. I successfully start it up, kick back the kickstand, roll away, ride conservatively down to the river. Find the Tower Bridge.

I park the bike. I run over to the railing. I can't believe this is happening. Terr must be kidding–we can work through it together. I know we can.

I scan the Thames. It's happening too fast; I feel dizzy. Hand on my abdomen. All I see is the heavy, greenish brown water, flowing, circles and eddies and ceaseless volumes of river water, heedless and unaffected by the calamity on its shorelines. Heading to the sea.

Then I see Terr, futzing around a small boat on the shore. I call out, wave, 'Terr, Terr, come back! You're making a big mistake!' I see him get into the boat, untie the line, the current takes the dinghy. It's like he doesn't hear me.

I'm screaming now, crying my eyes out, hand on the abdomen, crying for me and my child. For the dad.

'Terr don't leave me! Terr!'

He turns around and he spots me on the bridge. The boat is floating away. He doesn't even need an oar. The current goes quickly. He stands up in the middle of the boat. He waves with his right arm, long strokes back and forth. It's like an international distress signal, but with one arm.

Tears are streaming down. I can't believe this is happening. It seems rash, yet understandable in his quirky way.

Terr doesn't want to hurt me. Or the child. But my heart is broken. He's breaking my heart. He won't see me or the child anymore. We've been inseparable for the last year.

I stand at the rail, crying, waving, like at a departing soldier who I know will never come back.

The boat gets smaller, flowing in the middle of the Thames. He stands on the boat and waves. Arm flung back and forth, with feeling. It's still the same Terr, sick or no.

'Terr, don't leave me! Come back! Please Terr!'

I keep watching, the boat rapidly departing, toward...Nothing else in the Thames. The empty Thames, except for this lifeboat, and the now tiny figure waving.

'Terr, oh Terr. Don't do this! Come back!' I know there's no turning back. I stand at the rail, not keeping track of time. The Thames. The empty Thames.

CHAPTER 52: TWO WEEKS LATER

We've got me set up on a big cushy area. It's a platform above the nave, not far from the altar. We found blankets and pillows and velvet curtains, made a big pile, now I rest on a kind of soft, expansive throne. On my back; huge protuberant pregnancy. I feel like a beached whale, except that I lie in the ambient, reverent light of St. Paul's Cathedral.

Jesus and other iconic religious figures stare down at me from the heights. The best art London's religious elite could muster, before their own God forsook them.

I've been having contractions, really since Terr left. Small ones, like the thousands of earthquake tremors that precede the big one. Then, in the last day and a half, hard agonizing twinges. I cry out in pain. The boys are used to me now. First they came running every time, now they just sit cross-legged and watch me curiously.

They ask whether I need anything. They are attentive,

obedient, lacking in the nerves and tension of adults.

To them, it's an adventure. *Just wait to later on*, I think; they might not think it's so fun and novel anymore.

We have pots full of water distributed around the floor, sitting on the dais where I lie. I made them make a little fire outside and heat up the water. Once you get their attention, they are surprisingly useful. Their energy doesn't wane. Max is the best, a serious, obedient little boy. Maybe it's because he's Scottish.

Harry's been the tough one, trying to boss me around. He's oddly chauvinistic, for a little brat. Seems to think having a baby is no big deal. Walks around trying out names and trying to guess the sex, like he's my father-in-law.

Jack just follows Harry around. It's best to give them jobs to do, so they don't drive me crazy with their twisted, precocious male attitudes toward child-bearing.

Otherwise, they're attentive, know what's what, and will do anything I ask them to. Mostly adjust pillows and blankets and help me get up to pee, because I have to all the time now.

Only Max seems to understand the genuine gravity of the situation. He doesn't realize I could bleed to death during childbirth, or that the baby could be stillborn (really don't think that's going to happen, feeling the kicks all the time), or that other very bad outcomes are possible, but at least he's deferent and serious most of the time.

We're safe. I have help, food, companions. It's better than the train. Terr was wise, in his own way.

So we have pots of warm water arranged around me. Plenty of blankets and sheets (you'd be surprised how much linen a big church has). I've had lots of food from The Room, but not much of an appetite since Terr left. I eat sweets mostly; once, a sip of the red wine from a cut-glass chalice, to take the edge off.

Terr broke my heart, I think at idle times. When I'm not writhing in contractional pain. It was a decision he made. I'll just have to abide by it. I try not to think about it anymore. The implications, of when he said, 'I won't become one of them daft bastards!'

I wonder if he's floating in the Thames now. It's an awful image, simply terrible. I try to dispel it, think positive. Terr wouldn't do that, even though he swore he wouldn't become a daft bastard, a reiver.

I hold out remote hope I'll see him again. He knows where to find me.

The contractions are penetrating, longer lasting. I'd made the last entry in my journal three days ago, a journal piece addressed to Emma Blair Winslow (yep, that's the name, if it's a girl). I chose the name, not Terr's. I go by my gut. If it's a boy, Terry Blair Winslow.

I gave the journal to Max, told him to guard it with his life. I was going to tell him to give it to the child if I don't make it, but I didn't want to be so dramatic.

I don't sleep much now. A few hours here and there.

Then the contractions get really bad. Knifey, sharp, lengthy, right in that abdomen I've been caressing for months. I contort around on my back. I gave the boys only the barest of instructions.

I cry out, into the contractions. "Max, Harry, Jack! It's happening!" The thought arises, this could only be the prelude. I just don't know. They say the first pregnancy might be the easiest, because you don't know what's coming. This could go on for 24 hours, or more. I'll have to ride with it, whatever comes. For the sake of Emma or Terry.

"Shit! Christ!" He's staring down at me, in that soft church light. The eyes are empathic, a bit sad. At the moment, I don't feel an iota of religious detachment. I feel me and the baby, locked in a kind of mortal ordeal, us v. Mother Nature, who's never made this easy for women.

This ordeal, that's called survival. It's what I've been doing for the last couple of years.

A kind of aura, a black halo, forms just beyond my vision. I assume it means I might pass out. From the pain; then I start breathing. Rhythmically. I know to do that much. *Breath baby, breath!*

Raspy breaths and puckered lips, but it's working. Right through the contractions, the tectonic plates moving where my pregnancy is.

Just beyond the aura, I see Max, Harry, and Jack. Mouths agape, lips moving, words coming out. Stuff like "Are you okay? What do we do!"

"Get in front of my legs!" Which are spread. I hitch up my dress. The underwear's been gone for a while now. Welcome to life, boys.

"Gross!" I hear. "That's disgusting! What is that?"

"Probably the crown of the baby's head!" I gasp. Wishfully...

They're all gasping and recoiling. A scent rises, meaty like blood and fecund as in an odor rising from the wetlands. My water breaks. I sense it as a lake; it stains the sheets and curtain beneath me, and pools on some of that slatted wood flooring. Lake St. Paul's.

"What was that?" I hear Harry, scared to death.

"Just water!" I gasp.

"It's yellow!"

"That's okay! Take my word for it! Get more towels!" I scream in between the convulsive exhalations that widen the

210

black aura.

So it goes, for hours.

CHAPTER 53

I almost black out, in agony. The sheer lack of energy reserves. The blood loss, which is substantial enough that I can't look.

But I reach back into that void I've fallen into, like that dream when you step off into vast empty space, and I wrest back the control.

One boy on each leg, just as I told them. Pushing back. I need something to push against, but they don't weigh enough. They keep tumbling backwards.

I know the child is alive. I hear the boys shouting, yelling, as if from another room, hollering things more to themselves than me. Being boys.

"Touch it! Help it! No! Don't touch it! Get more bloody towels! Bloody Hell! Gross!"

Then I feel the completion of the child's laborious passage, emerging from the narrow birth canal. My cries carry through the church, the singing of a choir. I can only think of our train, moving through the spectral tunnel of King's Cross Station.

A great release, a profound lessening; a weightlessness, virtually like levitation.

"It's so red! The wrinkly face!" That was Max. "What is it? A boy!"

"No, it's not, you bloody wanker!" Harry. "It doesn't have a Johnny! See, she's a girl! Right there!"

I hold my breath. Seconds pass. Then I hear the crying, the wet bawling. This phenomenal, joyous wailing. The umbilical cord is soaked, heavy, foreign, like something big that was supposed to stay inside me.

Three boys, with their skinny arms and small hands. Holding her aloft. In the cathedral light that streams through a window. Emma.

CHAPTER 54

Dated: December 28, 2028

Dear Emma,

I wrote this before you were born. I knew you were a girl. Some women just know. But it's still weird addressing you as Emma, since that's my name.

I want to tell you a story.

There once was a girl who was born into a wonderful world called London. The only flaw in this place was a sickness around that was hard to cure. The girl never caught the sickness because of what she did.

She played in the grass and the dirt in the parks, and mud by the river when she bathed herself. She was outside all the time, whenever possible, soaking in the sun on her skin. Always, she got sun, during the day, even in winter.

She had three brothers. Her real father Terry had died a hero. Then three men—Harry, Jack, and Max—had acted like her brothers and played the role of father.

She ate all the good food they gave her to eat from the special place in the church. Some of that food was fresh, some of it was honey, garlic, and olive oil. She ate fish, eggs, and garden food. Gardens abounded in London; some of them had chickens behind the fence.

They ate vitamins and minerals every day.

She slept as much as she wanted to. She played all day, mostly outside. She was strong and lithe.

When they had the magic CBD oil, she took several drops under the tongue every day. Then they looked for more in the boundless empty pharmacies of the city.

They grew and harvested the magic cannabis plant in the gardens of London. She and the men planted seeds and grew it, inside and outside.

They dried the leaves and crinkled them up and sprinkled them into breads and oats and tea. This they did almost every day. This is how the girl never got the sickness, and neither did her men.

She grew to be older and strong, long reddish blond hair and wiry limbs.

The people who did get sick declined rapidly. She stayed away from them.

Never could they claim that she was the last female of her species. Because this wisdom of health and remedies in a sick time was passed down to others, and other girls and women emerged, and they in turn made healthy children with good men. Triumphantly.

I love you so much Emma.

Your Mum, Emma Wallace Blair.

215

Those were dark days, the first few ones after Emma was born. But they didn't last long, not after my milk started flowing. Emma suckled me and thrived. I could feel her gaining weight, under the blankets and against my chest and breasts.

The food from The Room was abundant; the scales were tipped in my favor.

We had a large stock of pilfered infant formula and food, along with my own milk.

The boys helped me staunch the blood flow in the beginning. Then it was a question of keeping the wounds clean down there. Days went by; a week. Emma continued to feed. But she had ripped me coming out.

I had no physician for a post-delivery surgery. No nurse midwife, to do an initial stitching, and to set me up with antibiotics.

I had three excited boys, and a newborn girl whose opening days were a struggle for survival.

Struggle has been the word for me, the context in which I've lived, since 2026.

I told the boys to go down to the river and look for Terr. I had this idea in my head that he was coming home.

Harry went out one morning and returned with a tale of a small dinghy tied to a pier not far from Tower Bridge. No people around it, though.

I realize I'm mildly delusional. It began with the odor wafting from the after-birth tears. I did everything I could to keep it covered. I splashed propylene glycol and whisky onto the wounds, crying out in pain. I salved it with honey, dripping from a wooden spoon, from The Room. To no avail. Some bacteria reign supreme, once they get their hooks into you.

At the turn of the century, the profligate use of antibiotics with people and livestock created a generation of superbugs, against which we have no strong defenses.

Emma, by this time, lies in a makeshift basinet, drinking milk from my breasts or from a bottle to which I've transferred some. She gets some store-pilfered formula as well.

I asked the boys to mount searches for anything containing CBD oil, including instructions on how to use it.

I was feverish. I made Hepburn sit down. I gave her a long pet, whispering to her. She's been by our side the whole time. I told her and the boys I'd be back soon. I took my small backpack, the trusty cricket bat, and went down to the Thames to look for signs of Terr.

EPILOGUE: 16 YEARS LATER

Dated: May 1, 2045

World population: Less than or equal to 100,000. London population: less than 1000.

My name is Emma Blair Winslow. I live in City Of London, in a restored home nearby St. Paul's Cathedral. I'm 16 years old. I live with my three brothers Max, Harry, and Jack.

Jack has a wife named Elizabeth. We all have different last names, because the men were orphaned by the plague, otherwise known as the Great Forgetting or as I prefer, the Barmy Fever.

I was born in the church not far from where an unordained minister now gives occasional sermons. Religion is marginally important for us, but we like to get together and sing and tell stories, not always on Sunday morning. It's mostly just the young folk, celebrating the morning sun and a new day.

We're like a tribe of hunter-gatherers or agriculturalists, but we take full advantage of and restore what was left of a large ultra-modern city, rather than simply living on grassy plains and in forests. We also spend much of our time cultivating gardens.

I reckon my birthday was January 3, 2029, or thereabouts. My three brothers were all there and rather cheekily take full credit for my birth and survival. As if it could have little to do with my dear Mum, Emma Wallace Blair.

Elizabeth, Max Ferguson's wife, is expecting in five months.

St. Paul's Cathedral, rather in my honor, also acts as a makeshift hospital; or at least I'm proud of the fact that I was the first "patient" there.

Harry says that makes me a kind of Third Coming, a female Christ. He says it was a miracle, me Mum could survive many depredations and bring me forth into that perilous world with little help, beyond the three boys.

Her own husband Terry Winslow eventually succumbed to the Barmy Fever. But he rode a motorcycle, fought coywolves, and did other amazing things, like get a ScotRail train running. I often think of him. Although I have no photo of Terry Winslow, Harry drew a picture for me of a man sitting on a motorcycle and smiling. I've concocted an image of him in my head, a big man proudly sitting astride his Harley.

What a holy reputation to foist upon a 16-year-old, just because I was born in a church! We don't have time in the London of 2045 for false deification. We do have some electric power, thanks to some clever engineering and hard work. The fact that we have any power, I'm told, from a combination of salvaged solar panels and siphoned gas and recovered propane for generators, is another sort of miracle.

People have also been able to power up my father's old train at King's Cross. People have studied it, and learned from its diesel-electric motor, enough to power up some of the other passenger cars. They're some of the largest lit-up machines you can see at night in London.

We have greenhouses, where we grow all kinds of vegetables and varieties of cannabis. The generators light the greenhouses and heat them when necessary, for we still have somewhat wet and chilly winters.

We capture rain in cisterns. In a pinch, we boil and filter Thames water. The Thames is much cleaner than before. There is no industry, large-scale farming, or massive populations (in London, 8 million before the Barmy Fever came) to pollute it.

The Thames receives clean rain; it's constantly refreshed.

Most of my time is spent in the greenhouses, planting, weeding, watering, harvesting. I like it. I feel productive. We need the fresh food, undoubtedly. No convenience stores and shops full of fast junk food.

We don't have formal schooling, probably because we don't have a large number of adults. We're a tribe of orphans. When kids and teenagers are largely in charge, there is no school.

That doesn't mean there's no reading or studying, because that's how I spend most evenings, when we're not singing, playing music, and goofing off around a bonfire.

I read everything I get my hands on, by candlelight. Of course, we have older survivors with technical knowledge who got the generators and the like going. They have younger apprentices. We gotta do that to survive.

Me and Elizabeth spend a lot of time cleaning up the house after Jack, Harry, Max, and our doggies Spencer and Hepburn II.

When all the infected people died, and my generation didn't catch it, H7N11 went dormant. It has subsided into dormancy, slipped into the woodwork as it were, but in all likelihood may still exist somewhere in the biosphere. It was still raging as of about 10 years ago.

We have no evidence that it's completely gone. No one touches the deer or other infected corpses, which have all been burned or buried. We use the wisdom contained in me Mum's diary, which has become a kind of cherished tale and bible. Everyone, or at least most people, live healthily under the sun, when it isn't cloudy, and liberally consume the cannabis in its many variations, for protection.

I'm the one who's responsible for editing and distributing me Mum's diary, of which hundreds of copies have been produced from the few working printers.

I heard stories about the coywolves in the city, my parents' battles with them. They died of the virus, or were hunted to zero. Same for the deer. The rabbits proliferate though, and don't get infected. They provide good meat.

We still get fresh water fish from the local rivers and the Thames; perch, pike, bream, roach, and more. Their populations have revived, since there are only a few hundred people fishing the river. There's tons of fish, and they don't carry as much mercury as before.

It goes without saying, we eat a lot of fish.

The generators power radios and we've gotten reports from Europe—Berlin, Geneva, Paris, Lisbon, and Madrid. Tribes of people are making steady progress. The pandemic isn't raging through humans anymore.

We're confident enough now so that small expeditions have traveled south. They take motorcycles, bicycles, and even boats across the Channel, or hiking through what's left of the

221

Chunnel, to connect with other humans on the mainland.

We can't always assume these southern tribes are friendly— the history books tell us that Europe was a warring land for a millennia or more. It was mostly migrations of new peoples taking over land from other humans. But we think it's important to make these face to face connections.

Whether or not we'll be a land of cars and jet airplanes again is doubtful though...Boats and vessels and maybe trains, yes.

The toys that people used before are museum pieces: wearable computers, cell phones, self-driving cars, robots that could replace joints and operate on peoples' hearts. They seemed the inventions of another species. When H7N11 took hold, they were obsolete in a matter of weeks. Poof...they were gone.

Computers are novelties. There are a few working ones around, in little command centers that have intermittent power and working servers. We can communicate with distant groups or tribes, but the widespread power doesn't exist to use a lot of machines. It has to be reserved for growing food.

We don't have the cell phones anymore. Duh! They are a relic from the past. I leaf through dog-eared magazines that have crinkled photos showing people toting, boastfully displaying, and typing into their cell phones. But I can't imagine always carrying this heavy, lit-up thing with me. What a waste of time, I think.

If I carry anything with me, it's me Mum's old cricket bat. It's a good luck charm. It has seven notches carved in it. The boys tell me they mark where she had to clobber the herded ones who came at her with the Barmy Fever.

People say Emma me Mum deserves a knighthood. Sir Emma Wallace Blair. Her theory about the binding of the

222

endocannabinoid system in the brain by H7N11, and the circumvention of the infection by using CBD and variations of cannabis extracts, and the building of robust immune systems with sun and antivirals as backups, has proven correct. It has worked for most people, and that's good enough for us.

The theory was revolutionary. Discovered outside of a lab and on the run, as it were.

Maybe the blokes down in Sweden–Stockholm is back on its feet in a small way, like London–will get around to giving out the Nobel Prize for Science again. If anyone deserves it, Emma does.

Harry says that me Mum survived the birth but got a germ "down below" that killed her in a month, not the Barmy Fever. They kept feeding me from a large store of formula. My Mum is buried in a cool, flowery place in Princess Diana Memorial Park.

I know from her journal that she speculated about being the last female human, alive and uninfected, on earth. Can you imagine that? Not only are you alone with your life hanging in the balance, but you carry the burden of the future survival of your species. Somehow, you manage to have a successful pregnancy, and give birth to a robust girl. Um, that's me.

I know for a fact that I'm not the last. No siree. That was one of Emma I's victories.

I will remember my Mum, who I never actually knew, for her more demonstrative qualities: the desire to persevere, to beat the odds, to retain a good humor, and most of all, to never give up. As Tennyson put it so well, "To strive, to seek, to find, and not to yield."

On Christmas, New Years, and April 1, her birthday, we all give pause and raise a wee dram of Scotch to her triumphant memory. Nothing by tradition will be sipped younger than a

15-year-old vintage (given availability, of course).

Last month, April 1, I raised my own glass on a crisp morning. Yes, I'll have a nip now and then in the morning, on special occasions. I imagine as she does it, back then alone, steadfast, seeing her own reflection in the sun's sparkle on the amber glass. 'To me, Emma.' Yes Mum, here's to you, I say, but silently. To you.

THE END